Creatures of the Moon

Kristine Overbrook

CRIMSON
ROMANCE
Avon, Massachusetts

This edition published by
Crimson Romance
an imprint of F+W Media, Inc.
10151 Carver Road, Suite 200
Blue Ash, Ohio 45242

www.crimsonromance.com

Dedication

FOR

BRIAN, MICHAEL, AND SHANNON

WHO DROVE ME TO THINK ABOUT WOLFING OUT IN THE FIRST PLACE.

I'D ALSO LIKE TO SAY THANK YOU TO TWO VERY SPECIAL WOMEN:

LAURA, FOR READING DRAFT AFTER DRAFT

JENNIFER, FOR GIVING CREATURES OF THE MOON A HOME.

Chapter 1

After six months, she'd have that murdering bastard locked down. In less than two hours things would be in place. She just had to handle one thing first.

"Alan, this isn't a good time." She moved the cell phone to her other ear and pulled her holster and weapon out of her desk drawer. Why did men always get clingy after three dates?

"It's never a good time for you, Lydia." Even over the phone she could see his disapproving scowl.

Struggling not to simply hang up, she pushed the button to switch the phone to speaker and sat it on her desk. "In case you forgot, I'm a cop; on call for stakeouts and killer catching."

The phone stayed silent as she strapped on her vest and settled her holster. Did he hang up? "Alan?"

"I had a night planned." His voice trembled. *Oh God, was he going to cry?* "It's our one-month anniversary."

She shifted her vest and stared at the phone. It should be a romantic gesture. Most women would love a guy who plans a special night. But all she could focus on was how the whine in his voice so closely matched nails on a chalkboard.

"Detective Davis?" Sergeant Eric Adams leaned into her office. "Ready?"

"Who is that?" Alan yelled. The tremor in his voice had turned hard. The scowl was back and something more. Something she wanted no part of. "Are you blowing me off for someone else on our anniversary?"

Lydia pinched the bridge of her nose and retrieved her cell from her desk, switching off the speaker as she did. She was about to lead a team of officers on a sting to catch a serial killer. The culmination of months of work. She didn't want to waste energy on this.

Adams cringed, but didn't appear at all contrite. She flipped him off then faced away from the door.

"Alan," she said, using the tone she reserved for frightened children. "You're right, this isn't fair to you. Go. Have a great life. I wish you all the best in the world."

"Wait—" She closed the phone on whatever would come next. Meaningless drivel or manly tirade, it would only make her late. Sometimes simply hanging up was best.

She tossed the phone on her desk and crossed the bullpen with Adams at her heels.

"Ready?" he asked.

"I've been ready to catch this guy for months."

*

"Is he in there?" Detective Lydia Davis asked as she approached the officers on scene.

She already had one officer down tonight. She couldn't let the bastard get away again.

"Yeah, we have two guys watching the rear," Sergeant Adams answered. "He hasn't come out yet."

The bastard was cornered now. She paused in front of a Cape Cod located in a quiet suburban neighborhood. It didn't fit the profile. Of course, this nut didn't fit any profile. Her men had pulled halfway into the driveway, blocking in an old brown station wagon. Maybe the killer's car? The smell of freshly cut grass filled her nostrils as she stood behind the SUV. Ah, the suburbs.

"Good." She didn't take her eyes off the house. "Could he have hostages in there?" she asked, anxious at the prospect of adding more casualties to the operation.

"No one went in with him. It's been for sale by owner for the last month and vacant."

"We can't wait for the rest of the team. Surprise is our best option." She took a breath, saying a silent prayer that she made the right choice. "Adams and you three, with me. The rest of you circle around and enter through the back of the house. Everyone be careful. This man is a savage."

She readied her weapon and moved past the station wagon to press against the yellow vinyl siding of the house. She and her team took positions in the flowerbeds lining either side of the door and waited several moments to allow the others to get into position.

After a silent count, she nodded to Adams and moved to open the door. Reaching for the knob, the loud report of a shotgun sounded from around back, echoing off surrounding houses, followed by measured shots from officers.

He was armed. *Not good.* But being under fire should distract him from the front and give her team the time they needed to enter. With adrenaline pumping, she fought to keep tight control of her emotions as she flung the door open and ran through, following closely behind Adams.

They entered into a front room left bare except for blinds and curtains over the front picture window. Motioning the other three to check the rest of the house, she and Adams moved through the room to the archway on their right.

This room was also completely empty. Not even dust gathered in the corners. In this room, however, the sweet smell of rotted meat filled her nostrils. She'd smelled worse, but it didn't bode well. She discovered another door to her left. This one appeared able to swing both ways.

The shotgun blasts were coming from behind that door. Lydia and Adams set up to enter. She motioned to Adams that she was going to look first. Bracing in anticipation of the horrors she may witness, she pushed the door open a crack. The smell of urine and ammonia burned her nose as she peered inside for an instant.

A beaker with tubes attached over a burner sat on a table in the corner. Boxes of sinus medicine and rat poison were stacked on the floor against the wall. Bags of what could only be crystal meth lay piled on the counter next to a set of old-fashioned scales.

Scanning, she caught sight of the killer. A very large man, about six foot two, stood in profile and glanced out the window of the back door, shotgun at the ready. Two inches of spotty growth covered his chin. His matted and greasy hair hung limp around his ears. Sweat and blood stained his clothes.

Then the man froze, ceasing his ragged growling gasps. His long nose sniffed the air as he turned. Barring his teeth in a vicious sneer, he swung the shotgun around and fired, blasting a plate-sized hole in the door.

As the door swung back from the blast, Lydia dropped to a knee, kept the door wedged open a second, and fired two rounds before spinning away. Both shots took the killer in the chest.

A scream that sounded more like a howl came from the murderer as he fired twice more. One shot took out the bottom corner of the door. The other exploded through the doorjamb inches from her elbow.

Adams caught the door on its swing and held it open for Lydia to take aim. Ferocious gunfire came through the back door. Again, she peered into the kitchen to see if the killer was down.

Pushed against the kitchen table by the gunfire coming through the rear entrance, the killer growled. His abdomen appeared riddled with wounds and blood streamed onto the floor, yet he still stood with his gun up and returned fire.

"Watch the beakers!" She yelled the precaution as she aimed for the man's head. One wrong move and they'd go up in flames.

The murderer turned at the sound of her voice. His ice-blue eyes locked with hers, and he grinned as she fired twice into his head.

The look in his eyes made her blood run cold. Even as his head rocked back, he let out a blood-curdling howl, but he just wouldn't go down. *God, how is he still moving?* He let the shotgun fall from his hands as he stepped toward her. His stare burned with a pleasure too focused to be drug-induced.

Again she fired, putting two more rounds into his skull. He fell on the table, hitting the lab. Flames exploded over the wall, spreading quickly. *Damn.*

"Get out of here!" Lydia ordered. Her officers moved out of the house, away from the flames and rolling black smoke. She glanced over her shoulder at the man she had tracked for months. Flames licked at his clothes as he lay in the wreckage. She'd wanted to bring him to justice, but that wasn't an option now.

You will be judged by a higher power today, she thought, as she exited amid a cloud of smoke.

The fire trucks had arrived. Lydia ran to the fire chief and reached out her hand. "You should know there was a meth lab inside and the body of our perp is in the kitchen."

The chief nodded and turned to do his job. She turned to her men, now gathered around their cars, waiting for her orders. The massive fire raging behind her illuminated their soot–covered faces.

It had been a long night. A quick head count told her she hadn't lost anyone else. Her men were proud, and the pleasure at taking this criminal off the streets was infectious.

She smiled. "Good work, guys."

"You got him, Davis," said Sergeant Adams.

"*We* got him," she corrected.

The other officers mirrored their grins, white teeth and eyes bright in the dimness of the evening, despite their fatigue. Their zeal improved her already good mood.

"Yup, no matter how hopped up he was, no way he walked out of there with a bullet in his head and covered in flames." She turned to look at the fire. It still raged, but the fire crews had it under control.

People crowded the nearby yards to view the spectacle. "Everyone loves to watch a fire," she muttered. She shook her head and ordered everyone to the precinct. With the exciting stuff over, they had paperwork to start. They grumbled as they headed for their vehicles. She chuckled and moved to her SUV.

"Lieutenant, can you make a statement?"

Lydia's shoulders slumped. Ryan Williams, a reporter for the *Daily Times*. Covering the murders, he'd dogged her every move for the last six months. She suspected he listened to his police scanner like most people listened to the normal radio.

She turned and looked up into a pair of magnificent green eyes. He stood several inches taller than her. He had long brown hair pulled into a loose ponytail and a closely trimmed beard, which made him look more like a biker than a prominent reporter.

A roguish smile played across his lips. "Were you able to apprehend the Bestial Butcher?"

She rolled her eyes. "Why do you insist on giving these whackos names? All it serves to do is raise them to the status of rock stars. It gives poor, twisted kids an avenue to stardom. *Oh, I'm gonna be bigger than Jack the Ripper.*" She gave Williams an icy glare and turned away.

"Did you get him?" His voice sounded strained.

She glanced over her shoulder. "I shot him between the eyes. He collapsed and set fire to himself and the house." She waved at the inferno. "No one could live through that. We'll be holding a press conference later if you want more information." She shook her head and escaped to her car.

*

Shaking off the effect of Detective Davis' eyes, brown streaked with gold, Ryan caught his breath. Her straight, light brown hair pulled into a no-nonsense ponytail at the nape of her neck swung slightly as she walked away. He enjoyed watching her walk. The view was a perk of following her around. She had an athletic body that confirmed the Pilates classes he'd learned she took three times a week.

He sought the same thing she did. He wanted the Butcher as much, if not more.

When he'd read several months ago that Lydia Davis was the detective assigned to the case, he knew she could track down the killer. He had to pull several strings, almost to the snapping point, to get the assignment.

The result pleased his boss. Because of the trouble the police had tracking the Bestial Butcher, several of his stories caused the paper to sell out hours after hitting the newsstand. People wrote in to give him hints and tips about who they thought the Butcher was and where they thought he hid.

Once he began passing on this information to the police, it became easier for Lydia to allow him to observe and question. She still didn't like him "tagging along," as she called it. However, she no longer threatened to arrest him when he showed up at a scene.

In fact, one of these tips started the action tonight. As the blaze consumed the remains of the house, Ryan scratched his chin thoughtfully. He climbed into his Jeep. He needed to get in place for the press conference.

*

Lydia eyed the collection of reporters waiting on the steps of the police station. Cameramen set up equipment along the back of a crowd. Reporters talked among themselves while they waited for her and the police chief to appear and step up to the bouquet of microphones that would catch their every word.

Inside, Lydia closed her eyes as she took a cool drink from a water fountain. Anything to quiet her shaking stomach. She hated this part of her job. She could handle a group of officers, the chief, or a stone-cold killer, but every time she stood in front of a group of reporters, she shook like a leaf.

"Simple stage fright. Nothing to worry about. You'll get used to it," they'd told her when she first made detective.

She'd been a detective for five years, and her stomach still did acrobatics when she had to talk in front of a large crowd. Taking a deep breath, she pushed the butterflies into a tight ball. Then she stood ready to face the cameras.

The chief of police, a short, balding man with salt-and-pepper hair and mustache, stomped down the hall in her direction. Although he couldn't weigh more than 145 pounds soaking wet, Chief Fairweather waddled like a man three times his size.

An injury when he worked vice forced him to desk duty. His dedication to the force and his reputation for honesty got him elected as chief of police. He had an evident air of authority as soon as he entered a room.

As he approached Lydia, he winked. "Let's do this," he said. He was a great man.

She accompanied him through the doors, and the assembled mass of reporters quieted.

The chief stepped to the microphones. "Okay, the criminal known as the Bestial Butcher is presumed to be dead, killed in a shootout when my detective and several officers attempted to apprehend him. It also appears he was a drug dealer. As we speak, the fire department is putting out a blaze that destroyed him and the vacant house where we believe he's been living. Once the fire is completely out, we'll have forensic teams going over the area, and the coroner will remove and inspect the body."

He looked out over the reporters' heads, directly into the cameras. "Because of the dedication of the police force, another criminal is off the streets." Again, he looked at the reporters. "We will now field questions."

The reporters clamored. The chief pointed to a woman from Channel Sixteen News.

"So, how many people were victims of the Butcher?"

"So far, we can attribute twenty-four slayings to him. Once his body is in the coroner's office, DNA will be taken, and we will try to match other homicides to the Butcher."

"Can you give us some background on the killings?"

Lydia glanced at the chief, and at his nod, she responded. "At first, the laceration patterns on the victims appeared as if an animal had attacked them. In fact, after the first victim, police assumed they looked for a rabid animal." Through act of sheer will, she kept her limbs from betraying her nerves.

"Only after the body count increased did homicide get called in; the killer was human. He hunted in an area too widespread for an animal to traverse. Several victims were attacked inside their apartments. We considered it unlikely a rabid dog would manage to go up five flights of stairs to attack a single individual in a secured building."

More clamoring, then a man from CNN asked, "Is it true that all of the victims were women?"

Lydia answered, "No. In fact, there were several men. There was no discrimination in affluence, race, or sex. This, in particular, made it difficult to profile the killer."

The same man asked, "What led you to believe you could make an arrest this evening?"

"We had a tip that he might strike again. During the stakeout, he appeared and attacked an officer, who was acting as bait." Everyone started talking and Lydia raised her hand. "The officer wore protective gear and is in the county hospital with his family. He is doing fine."

A man with the *Times* asked, "From whom did you get this tip?"

The chief stepped forward. "C'mon, Dave, you know most tips are anonymous."

The conference continued with the reporters asking more questions about the victims and motives of the Butcher. The butterflies in Lydia's stomach once again took flight. She shifted uncomfortably. Surely this couldn't go on much longer. She scanned the journalists and noticed Ryan Williams. He stood at the far edge of the crowd, holding up a mini recorder. A flush warmed her face. Perhaps with the case over they could go out for drinks or dinner or—

"And have you already been assigned another case, detective?"

Still looking at Williams, Lydia startled at the question. She stammered at the reporter who spoke. "Um . . . My next case . . ." She glanced at Ryan and he winked. "Um . . ."

The chief gave Lydia an amused look. "The detective will be going on a well-deserved vacation."

Surprised, she somehow managed a smile and a nod.

"All right, everyone, thank you and goodnight." He lifted a hand in a wave, then touched Lydia's elbow. She followed him through the doors.

"What the hell was that?" he muttered under his breath as they walked to his office. "That was the most vacant expression I have ever seen. And I have never seen one on you." Walking three feet ahead, he missed Lydia's shrug.

"Sorry, I spaced out for a second." She entered his office. The only thing that distinguished it from hers was the sign on the desk, "Harold R. Fairweather, Chief of Police."

"Look, Davis." He motioned for her to sit as he rounded the desk and did the same. "I know you haven't slept for six months."

She rolled her eyes.

"I'm serious about the vacation. Take a couple days off. Go visit friends. Get a spot on the beach. Heck, sit around in your bathrobe and veg at the television for hours on end. I don't care. But you're not going to start a new case until you recoup."

"Chief—" she started to protest.

"I mean it. Don't argue with me. Get out. See you in three days." He picked up her case report and a pen. He made a show of reading for a bit, then looked at her. "You still here?"

Lydia smiled. "No, sir. Just left." She exited, shaking her head.

He took care of his force. Everyone commented on how talking to him was like talking to a father. She didn't remember hers, having transferred from foster home to foster home most of her life.

Shaking off emptiness, she headed to her office to grab her things. As she mulled over what to do with her newly acquired time, she smiled. First thing would be to soak in a hot bath.

"Taking a vacation?" Sergeant Adams looked up from his desk. When she gave him a quizzical look, he explained, "E–mail already went out."

"I've been ordered to take a couple of days off." She shrugged.

"Any plans?"

"I hadn't really thought much beyond getting cleaned up."

Adams laughed. "Make the most of it. Go somewhere you don't have to think too much."

Lydia chuckled as she went into her office and grabbed her tattered backpack from the corner where she'd tossed it three days ago. She'd lived out of her pack on more than one occasion.

Driving home, she wondered what she would do for her vacation. She really needed peace and quiet, somewhere outside the city. Maybe spend a couple days hiking or fishing. No neighbors thudding on the walls or sirens screaming down the street. And where the loudest sounds were birds tweeting. She smiled. Three days might be enough to unwind.

*

Ryan turned away as the press conference ended. He enjoyed seeing Lydia flustered. She controlled herself so well that he took great pleasure in baiting her. In his work, he'd dealt with plenty of detectives, and usually he had fun irritating them. They had a sense of importance third only to doctors and lawyers. They all took themselves so seriously. He couldn't help poking holes in their inflated egos.

Lydia proved more fun because she was beautiful when she got angry. Her eyes flashed and her cheeks flushed and . . . *Simply fantastic.*

At his Jeep, he paused, mulling over asking her to dinner. He wanted to grab a bite, and the way she'd reacted at the press conference made him think perhaps she would say yes.

"And then what?" he said aloud to no one as he got in and started the engine. He saw no real future for them.

How could he explain what would happen when they had their first fight? No, a working relationship was better for both of them. He turned on the radio and sang along to a rock song as he drove home.

As fate would have it, he lived across the street from Lydia's building. Well, not exactly fate. He'd moved into the furnished apartment once he found out she was the detective working the Bestial Butcher case.

Since their first meeting, he felt compelled to protect Lydia. She had no real idea what she had gotten involved in. Although he had no doubt she could deal with society's scum with dispatch, the Bestial Butcher was not society's typical scum.

Entering the apartment, he tossed his keys onto the coffee table. He walked to the refrigerator and opened a can of tomato juice. As the thick, tangy liquid flowed down his throat, his mind wandered.

Prowling night streets looking for the Butcher had led him to tracks only the Butcher could leave. Lydia would follow up on the tip he'd passed her. She had to.

He tossed the empty can in the recycle bin and plopped on the sofa. Although the apartment came furnished when he started leasing it, he wouldn't have decorated it any other way. Heavy furniture boasted solid wood and upholstery stuffed to overflowing. In the case of a very comfortable blue recliner, white filler peaked through seams on one side whenever someone sat in it.

Taupe walls gave the room a feeling of warmth. Neither the recliner nor the faded orange sofa matched the hunter green shag carpet or brick-colored curtains that covered a street–view picture window. Yet the place had a coziness about it. Aside from the perfect view into Lydia's apartment, the ambience had influenced his reason to live there.

His tastes had not always tended toward homey. He remembered a time when he preferred deco furniture and open space. Only in the past few years had his tastes changed to a cozier den-like atmosphere.

He closed his eyes and stretched. In the morning, he would go to the station and see what information he could get out of them about the condition of the Butcher's body... if they even found a body. He knew somehow that the Butcher hadn't died. Not even in that fire. And if he lived, the Butcher had escaped unseen. Even with all the firefighters surrounding the house and onlookers watching from the street. Next time, he would need to get to the scene sooner if he wanted to catch him.

Having that animal slip through his fingers again built a familiar rage. Knowing this emotion all too well, he rose from the couch and stood in the middle of the room with his arms outstretched. As he slowly bent to touch his fingers to the floor, the burning in his gut began to recede. He held the posture for another few moments and moved on to the warrior.

Long ago, he'd learned to control his anger with yoga. Of all the stress–reduction and anger–management techniques he'd tried, including medication, yoga worked the best. At times, he could not completely control the crazed anger that washed over him. During these times, he was glad he didn't own the furniture and didn't intend to regain his security deposit. He had kept all his real possessions in storage for the past three years.

His life had turned upside down then. He'd almost gone insane with pain and anger. Luckily, he regained his lucidity before destroying anything he valued. Once he placed his things in storage, he started his quest to track down the cause of his life's upheaval, which led him to the city and to Detective Lydia Davis. He moved into the lotus position with a smile on his face. She was something else.

She struck a chord in him that, up until they met, he did not realize existed. Oh, there had been women—some short relationships and, of course, a few one-night stands. However, in the past three years, women had held no interest for him.

That all changed when he first saw Lydia. Something awoke. It yearned for her in a primal way. It was much more than sexual, although he wouldn't mind spending several hot, sweaty nights with her.

Ryan rose from his position on the floor. The direction of his thoughts sapped the anger out of him, but his heart rate was way up. To get any sleep, he would have to spend twenty minutes under a cold shower. He went to the window to close the drapes, but took a moment to gaze toward her apartment.

A small light shone in her bedroom, and although she had drawn the shade, he could see her faint silhouette as she moved around the room. His breath caught in his throat at the sight of her. Then she stopped and started to undress, pulling off her shirt.

"Oh God," he whispered out loud, gripping the drapery with both hands. The shade did nothing to hide the roundness of her breasts as she turned, bent, and then lifted her arms over her head to allow the fabric of a nightshirt to slip over her body. She moved to the right and turned off the light.

Only after the room across the street darkened did Ryan start to breathe again. He let out the air with a shudder and released his grip on the drapes. It took every bit of his self-control to push aside the idea of going over there and knocking on her door. How he longed to caress that body. He shook his head, wanting to knock the image from his mind's eye. Finally, he turned in a daze and stalked to the bathroom and that cold shower.

Chapter 2

The next morning, Lydia stood in the bedroom of her apartment. There was nothing special about her room. Most of her apartment tended toward serviceable, not homey.

Lydia wasn't a pack rat. With a childhood spent jumping from family to family, she learned not to get attached to anything because it could be gone as fast as it came. Therefore, she liked to keep things simple.

No heavy credenzas or antique dining room tables. Most people got these treasures from family. Having none, and not remotely interested in starting a family of her own, she was in no hurry to acquire *things*.

One treasured item, a silver leaf pendant she always remembered having and managed to keep throughout her travels, hung from a string on the corner of her dresser mirror. The pendant had engravings etched in black over the front; they almost looked like writing. As a young girl, she would sometimes sit alone and imagine what the carvings meant. Her favorite theory was that they carried a message of devotion, a way of bonding two souls.

Without realizing, she picked up the pendant and crossed the room to the window. The silver glinted in the morning sun coming through the curtains.

A siren screaming down the street woke her wandering mind. She sighed, replaced the pendant, and turned to the bed where she considered her empty backpack.

Finally, she tossed in some appropriate clothes, then the first-aid kit she'd purchased on the way home from the office. Knowing anything could happen while camping alone, she didn't want to take chances. A hairbrush, toothbrush and other toiletries, waterproof matches, cooking kit, and finally some packages of camping food went into her pack. Then she tied her sleeping bag and tent to its outside.

She hoisted it to her shoulders, hefting a couple of times, but stopped short of walking out the door. She sensed something missing. Her gun. It didn't feel right to leave the house without it. On the other hand, she had no reason to wear it since she had no plans to hunt squirrels. A handgun would do her no good in the woods.

But she never left the house without it, putting it on in the morning like most women put on makeup. Finally, she took off the pack and strapped on her weapon under her light coat. This time when she put on the pack, it felt right. Smiling, she headed downstairs for her coffee.

*

Her apartment building sat atop The Shop, a coffee–pastry store. She enjoyed the smell of brewing coffee and freshly baked muffins every morning. Rich, calming scents that helped focus her mind and ready her for the day. On a normal morning, she would take her bagel and cappuccino to a corner booth and read the paper. Not a morning person, this proved a great way to wake up.

They knew Lydia well and had her "usual" ready moments after she appeared for breakfast. Today, she asked them to bag it for her.

Sipping her cappuccino-to-go, she drove her SUV out to a campground several hours outside of the city. Passing through the first half of the area dedicated to RVs, she snorted as she drove past. She saw no point in going camping if you took your house with you. If they could watch television and use a microwave, they weren't camping.

She delighted in the beautiful day. Sunlight filtered through leaves, and the fresh fragrance of nature carried on a breeze. The pines, leaves, grass, and earth were a sharp contrast to those scents that filled her every day. About a mile from the RVs, Lydia pulled into a parking area designated for campers who wanted to hike to a site. Two other cars occupied spaces: a light-blue station wagon and a black compact.

Energized by the fresh air, Lydia pulled her pack out of her car. Though hours from the city and well away from the RV families, she decided to hike further still from any possible encroachment of her solitude.

As she started into the woods, she knew she grinned like a fool, but she couldn't help it and didn't want to. Camping relaxed her. It was an activity where she had a say, where she was in control.

She'd searched for control in other ways too, throwing herself into her work. Even in school her teachers called her an avid student, and she deplored the idea of having to go without class for two whole months in the summer. Of course, moving to a new foster home had meant she would almost always have to change schools, so fortunately, she spent many summers in the classroom, catching up on work. The distraction allowed her to concentrate on subjects she could understand, and not the intricacies of playground politics. Now, as an adult, she needed to ensure she had everything finished before she shifted her attention to the next project or assignment.

She turned off the main, hard–packed path to follow what looked like a game trail. Leaves and twigs crunched under her boots, and the occasional branch caught on her sleeve. Stepping over a rotted log, she ducked so her pack would not get caught in the low branches of a red maple tree.

Some people called her compulsive. Maybe they had it right. She found it wrenching to leave a task incomplete.

This brought her mind back to the Butcher case. They'd not given his body a full autopsy when she'd left. Though she would return to work by the time the lab completed DNA evaluations, it seemed wrong to take a vacation, even under orders, while aspects of the case remained undone. She should be in her office, pacing anxiously for the results.

Although, when the chief ordered her to take a vacation, she only objected for a moment. She enjoyed activity and a change of scenery. Still, something in her gut said she should return to the station. Brushing off the notion, she continued her trek.

In a small clearing, two deer grazed. They lifted their heads when she cleared the trees. Her breath caught in her throat. They stood so close. No matter how often she hiked, she would never tire of viewing animals in their natural habitat—almost a religious experience.

Impulsively, she moved toward them. Already on alert, they bounded through the trees. Living nature in every form thrilled her; her heart leapt along with the deer. She lowered herself to sit on a fallen tree, closing her eyes to see them again.

Her pack started to weigh on her, and she realized she had lost a sense of time. How long had she sat on the log? When she opened her eyes, she decided the glade would make the perfect place to camp. She shrugged off the heavy pack and started about setting up her tent.

*

Lydia stared into bright, dancing flames. *Even I like to watch a fire.* She finished eating a fish she'd caught in a nearby stream. Now sitting propped against a stump, she gazed dreamily into the flames, enjoying the sizzle–pop as the logs succumbed to the blaze. Months of tension eased from her shoulders and neck as the comforting warmth radiated through her body.

With only her thoughts for company, her mind wandered to Ryan Williams. He'd followed the Butcher case intently. Every time a call came in about another possible victim, he emerged from the woodwork, notebook in hand. Sometimes bombarding her with questions, sometimes watching and trying to catch conversation.

She closed her eyes and relived the first time she'd met him.

Lydia pulled up to the scene of another savage killing. Crossing crime scene tape, she approached a forensic team hovering over shredded remains of a body.

"By the smell, this one's been here a while." Lydia put the back of her gloved hand to her nose. "Okay, what can you tell me?"

A woman stood and walked over. "Black female, around forty I would guess, but we won't really know more until we get her into the lab." She removed her gloves and shook Lydia's hand. "Castillo."

"Davis."

"Look, Davis, I've been doing this for a long time so I've seen all kinds of carnage. If I didn't know better, I'd say this was done by a rabid animal."

"Castillo, I have heard this before, it—"

"I know, the range is too broad. I know that," she said through gritted teeth. "Just look at this." She led Lydia over to the body, pulling on a fresh pair of gloves as she went. She crouched and motioned for Lydia to do the same.

The body sprawled face down on the ground. Lydia could tell the woman had attempted to flee her attacker. When she'd fallen, he must have pinned her because she'd tried to pull free. The victim's right hand still gripped the grass past her head, although the arm it attached to had been completely severed at the shoulder. Other than that, the skeletal structure of the body stayed intact, despite its severe mutilation. Not an inch of skin remained on the back. The organs had been ripped aside, and Lydia could see turned earth through the hole.

"See this?" Castillo pointed to the victim's calf. "What do you make of that?"

"Looks like tooth marks to me," said a deep voice.

Lydia looked in the direction of the unfamiliar voice. A man in a sports coat and jeans stooped by the victim's feet.

"Who the hell are you?" Lydia and Castillo demanded together.

"Ryan Williams, *Daily Times*." He extended a hand.

Lydia stood and took it, and then half led, half dragged him back across the tape. "This is a crime scene, Mr. Williams. Cross this tape again and I will throw you in jail." She stared at him, hoping to see that he understood. Instead he regarded her with the oddest expression.

"Triumph," Lydia whispered. She remembered that he'd been extremely pleased with something, but she couldn't place the reason why.

She stood to put more wood on the fire and froze at a rustling in the trees nearby. Instinctively reaching for the gun still strapped under her coat, she hesitated to pull it, not wanting to shoot a hiker. She stared into the darkness. After a long minute, a large beast moved through the woods. Another moment and it came into the glade.

She shook her head and removed her hand from her weapon. The deer had returned. Very slowly, so as not to startle it, she sat. Laughing inwardly at her jumpiness, she reached into her pack and took out a chocolate chip cookie. As she brought the morsel to her lips, the deer lifted its head, its tail raised in alarm, and it bounded away.

A fierce growl echoed around the glade. Before Lydia could drop the cookie and pull her gun, it leapt on her. Pain seared her right shoulder as the beast bit. Claws raked her legs, and the momentum pushed her onto the ground beside the stump she'd leaned against a second before.

She tried to push the animal off. It released its grip on her shoulder, and she felt gashes open across her cheek and nose. She choked down the searing pain and fear, and she struggled to focus on her defense. Her left arm rose to protect her face. The beast wrapped its mouth around her arm and shook its head like a dog with a rag. Lashing out with her feet, she bucked and groped for her gun.

Cold metal pressed against her back where her shirt had ridden up. With great effort, she reached with her right hand, her left arm now useless. Her fingers slid around the grip, years of training coming to the fore and overshadowing the pain. She lifted the weapon and fired into the fur.

The beast barely yelped. She fired again. It released her arm. She shot again and again and again. Screams filled the air. Her vision swam and her strength ebbed. She was losing blood.

Another large creature leapt into the clearing.

"No," she whimpered. Her strength completely gone, her gun fell from her fingers.

Blackness.

*

A wet cloth dabbed her forehead. Lydia groaned and stretched. Someone gently lifted her head and stuffed a soft pillow under it. She opened her eyes to see Mrs. Holly sitting on the edge of a cot, holding a cool cloth to Lydia's head.

She lay in her third grade nurse's office.

No. This wasn't right. Her vision swam and the kind face wavered as tears ran down her cheeks. Lydia was an adult, but the pain made it easy to submit to the nurse's ministrations.

"Easy now. That was a nasty bump. You say you fell?" Mrs. Holly leaned close to look into her eyes.

"Yes, um . . . " That day so long ago in the third grade came back in a flood of memory. The other children had pushed her off of the jungle gym, laughing and teasing because she had no real parents.

Mrs. Holly's eyes narrowed, still staring into Lydia's eyes.

God, she doesn't believe me. If I tell, they will just do worse to me.

More tears welled on her lids. Her chest hurt with the pain of overwhelming emptiness. So lonely, *but maybe alone is better.*

Her body quaked and pain ripped through her shoulder. Gashes opened in her shirt and spurted blood on Mrs. Holly.

Horrified, Lydia gripped her shirt and stared at the school nurse. Mrs. Holly started to swell, and her nose and mouth stretched into a muzzle. Dark brown fur sprouted all over her body.

The creature climbed onto Lydia's cot and crouched over her legs. She tried to call for help, but she could only gurgle in fear. The creature opened its mouth, showing blood-covered teeth in an odd grin. Then it lunged.

*

Lydia moved faster than humanly possible. Leaves barely crunched under her paws as she ran through the forest. Weaving through trees, she sensed her prey lingered nearby. Its beacon of scent called to her.

Her powerful body moved fluidly toward her quarry. Firelight shone through the trees. Lydia slowed her pace. She could smell it intensely now. She circled the ring of light and located her prize. A woman sat against a tree stump, facing the fire.

Every fiber of her being longed to rip into the woman's flesh. Lydia could barely contain herself. She edged closer, inching toward the clearing. The woman reached into a bag beside her. With unbound joy, Lydia roared as she bounded across the remaining distance and sank her teeth into her own shoulder.

Chapter 3

Ryan dressed quickly the next morning and whipped up a protein drink for the road. As he poured the concoction into a travel mug, he wondered if Lydia managed to get any sleep before the station called her about the missing body.

At his Jeep, he glanced across the street for Lydia's car. *It's not there. She should be back at the station by now.*

Putting the travel cup in a holder, he sped to find her. No way had the fire actually killed the Butcher.

When he arrived at the precinct, the calmness of the place astonished him. At the very least, he expected more reporters. Hadn't Lacy from Channel Six planned to camp on the precinct steps so she could get the best position for statements on the autopsy results?

Just inside, he came to a security checkpoint. Ryan walked through the metal detectors as the guard on duty sniffed his travel mug.

"Berries?" The guard handed back the drink with an amused expression.

"I just can't stomach the soy stuff first thing in the morning. Why, want some?" He took a long drink. "Yum," he said with a grin.

Chief Fairweather's voice boomed, "Mr. Williams, I would've thought you'd be with the other reporters at the hospital."

Ryan turned and greeted the chief with a warm handshake. "Good morning, sir. They're making the statement at the hospital?"

"Yup." Fairweather took a sip from a coffee mug. "The doctors plan to make a statement on the condition of Officer Jacobs at the same time."

"Oh. Guess I should get over there." Ryan stood on unsteady ground all of a sudden. Where was Lydia?

"Just a minute, Williams. Lydia's report said you provided the tip that led us to the Butcher."

"Yeah, well the paper was getting tips and I just passed them on."

A secretary stepped into the hallway. "Chief, there's a call for you from the hospital." From the thin set of her mouth, Ryan could tell the call meant bad news.

"Without you, we couldn't have set up the sting last night." The chief clapped Ryan on the shoulder and left to take the call.

Ryan finished off his breakfast, curiously waiting to hear bad news. After a moment, when no outburst or other reaction came from the chief's office, he started toward the exit.

"What!" boomed the chief's voice.

Ryan stopped in his tracks. *Here it comes.*

"Well, get on it! Get crews out there and comb the area. Process the scene again. Catalog everything!" Several thuds sounded before the chief emerged from his office and yelled into another set of offices. "Adams!"

"Yes, chief!" came a prompt response along with the loud, abrupt scraping of a chair.

"Find Davis. Get her back here. Now!"

Find Davis? Where the hell is she? Ryan thought.

"Yes, chief."

Chief Fairweather turned to enter his office and stopped when he spotted Ryan. "Forget the hospital. The Butcher's body wasn't in the wreckage of the house."

Never forgetting his duty as a reporter, he quickly asked, "May I quote you on that, sir?"

"Why the hell not? The damn doctor told the reporter that no body came in last night. Said he'd have someone call them as soon as he had something to tell." He turned. "Adams, where the hell is Davis?"

Yeah, where the hell is Davis? Ryan echoed.

"No answer at her house or cell, sir. She left a voicemail saying she planned to go camping. She must've left already. With those hills, she might not get cell service."

"Do you know which campground she went to?"

"No, sir."

Chief Fairweather mumbled a string of words Ryan couldn't make out, but he bet they could blister paint. The man stormed into his office.

With his heart in his throat, Ryan returned to his Jeep. Although he'd suspected the Butcher still lived, he hadn't worried that Lydia was in danger until the chief couldn't reach her. The Butcher would hunt her now that she posed a threat.

*

Ryan sped to her apartment. The Butcher could track her. People like him had unconventional resources. The ride home seemed to take forever, which worked to his advantage. When his blood started to boil, his perceptions heightened—one of the few benefits of the incident three years ago.

He parked in a space a block away and wove his way through the press of people. When he arrived at the door to her building, he punched the code to enter. He had watched her long enough to learn it. After racing up the stairs, he knocked on her door. It swung open slowly. *Damn.*

He entered cautiously. His eyes searched the room, and he tilted his head to listen for the slightest noise. Sniffing, he detected an odor of musk and soot mingled with the fragrance of an air freshener plugged into an outlet in the living room. The Butcher had been there.

The room was trashed. What furniture she owned, the Butcher had smashed and shredded. The contents of the kitchen cabinets cluttered counters and the floor. He frowned. Something about the destruction seemed odd.

What purpose had that criminal served by trashing her apartment? Once the Butcher realized Lydia's absence, why didn't he lay in wait for her? Why did it look as if he searched for something? Ryan moved from room to room, scanning for anything unusual. Every room was in disarray.

Her bedroom held an extra surprise. Apparently, the Butcher wanted to leave a sign that he would be back. Her bed lay stripped, the mattress soaked. The smell overpowered him. Urine.

Perhaps he did it to mark his territory. Whatever the reason, she wouldn't be able to use the bed again. A pile of her clothes and the bedding sat next to the dresser. It appeared as though the Butcher had rolled in it. Several stray hairs stuck to the pile.

Such behavior might seem strange for a normal person, but Ryan knew who and what he chased. This was perfectly in character. Well, at least they could get DNA samples.

As Ryan made to leave, he couldn't shake his disappointment. No evidence pointed to where Lydia had gone. Then in the living room, he found it—a balled pamphlet in a corner with the word "camp" visible in green.

Ryan retrieved and smoothed it. His instincts told him she had gone to this place. About four hours outside of the city, they allowed tent camping and offered hiking trails. After studying the map on the back for a moment, he again wadded the paper and returned it to its place in the corner.

The Butcher had been in the apartment; he knew where to find Lydia. Ryan swallowed the fear that rose in his throat. The Butcher could be going after her for two reasons, and neither one of them was good. Ryan had to find her first.

On his way downstairs, he considered calling the police and telling them her location. He discarded the idea almost as soon as he thought it. They would want to know how he knew, why he didn't tell them when he visited the office earlier, and how he knew where she lived. Questions he would rather not answer.

*

Ryan pulled into the rather empty parking area of the campground as the sun began to set. The entire trip, he stayed on edge. He had to get to her before the Butcher did. What would he say when he found her? *Fancy meeting you here? Okay, it's official. I'm an idiot.* He ran over every possible scenario in his mind.

He found Lydia's car and parked his Jeep next to it. He got out and breathed the forest air. Standing beside her vehicle, he caught a whiff of her shampoo. His sheepish smile at catching her scent quickly melted, replaced by the realization that if he could smell her, so could the Butcher.

He scanned the area but couldn't see anyone or anything nearby. In the woods, he proceeded carefully so as not to snap twigs and alert anyone to his presence. He followed the wonderful aroma of her shampoo.

He moved somewhat hunched, and although his hands never touched the ground, he longed to run on all fours. Too hard to explain away if he encountered somebody, he chose instead to slink through the trees just off the path. Every so often, he returned to it, making sure he stayed on her trail.

After several minutes, he caught another scent. Musky. Like a wet dog, but with another odor layered in. Soot. The Bestial Butcher was here. If he had not already identified that scent in Lydia's apartment, he may have dismissed it for a camper's pet that rolled in old campfire ashes.

Lydia faced grave danger. Ryan saw no alternative except to assume his other form.

Ryan growled as he placed his hands on the ground. His body wrenched as it shifted into that of a wolf. It was not as painful as in the beginning, three years ago. In fact, now it felt almost like stretching.

In this form, he could *see* the scents around him. Lydia's appeared a robin's egg blue. Overlapping it floated an insidious dark green that indicated the Butcher followed her as well, waiting for the right moment to strike. At this realization, Ryan moved off at a silent run through the forest, bounding over fallen logs and dodging trees with quiet ease.

Through the forest, he heard a growl and then a scream. Too late! He put forth another burst of speed, swiftly moving around obstacles. Another log. A bush. A deer bolted out of nowhere and bolted over him.

Gunshots rang through the woods from just ahead. He burst from the trees and hurled himself onto the hairy back of the staggering beast. Ryan sank his fangs into its flesh and yanked its head back.

Blood spurted and claws reached around in an attempt to dislodge him. They pierced the skin of his neck. Suddenly the beast flipped him onto the ground and it leapt atop him.

Ryan stabbed his claws into the beast's abdomen just as teeth closed on his throat. Instead of the crushing bite he expected, the Bestial Butcher threw his head back in a howl of pain.

Using this opportunity, Ryan pushed his way to a standing position and slashed at the Butcher's neck. Blood gushed from the wound. The beast grabbed its throat with one clawed hand and made to slash at Ryan with the other, but at the last minute, it ran into the woods.

Ryan roared in frustration and started after it. However, a frightened moan behind him caught his attention.

Lydia lay on the ground, her gun in the grass next to her. Her eyelids fluttered. Puncture wounds on her shoulder glistened in the firelight. Ryan cursed. The beast had bitten her.

Tonight she would start her transformation. Ryan shook his head and knelt by her blood-covered body. In that moment, he knew he would have to get closer to her than he'd ever hoped.

Chapter 4

Lydia woke slowly from a fitful sleep. Her body ached, and she rolled over in her soft sleeping bag. The intense pain in her shoulder overpowered the throbbing in her head. Gingerly, she opened her eyes. Backlit by the sun, the tent wall glowed green. She was used to this phenomenon; however, something still did not feel right somehow. She rubbed her eyes in an attempt to ease the pain behind them.

The smell of damp canvas overpowered all the other scents of the forest around her. Her backpack waited in a corner. Next to her head sat her canteen. She reached for it and lifted her head slightly to drink. It took several mouthfuls before the reason for the unfamiliarity hit her. She didn't remember bringing her things inside the tent. Nor did she recall going to bed.

She sat up straight. A wave of dizziness overcame her from the sudden movement, and she nearly vomited. Dropping her canteen and closing her eyes, she pressed her temples. After several long minutes, she regained control and took another glance around in the greenish light.

All of her belongings were arranged neatly around the tent just so, as she had done many times on past camping trips. She sat in the middle of everything, wracking her sieve-like brain for any clue as to how she got to bed last night.

She remembered fishing, sitting by the fire. She strained to conjure more memory. Flashes of the attack returned to her. With every throb of her still-aching head, another moment of time returned.

She reached for her injured shoulder and found it encased in bandages. She unzipped and slipped out of her sleeping bag to examine the wounds she remembered receiving to her legs. They were also bandaged in long strips of cloth that looked ripped from a T-shirt.

Out of the fog of her dreadful headache and pieced-together memories, she concluded that she could not have done this for herself. Was the person who did this still nearby? The idea that someone lurked close sent chills down her spine.

Instinctively, she scanned the tent for her gun. She found it behind her pack. A look in the clip at the reassuring bullets soothed her, and the aches seemed to fade. The weight of the metal in her hand comforted her. As an afterthought, she pulled a shirt and shorts from her pack and changed gingerly.

She opened the tent flap, unzipping it slowly to minimize noise. Steeling her nerves, she stepped out of the tent and swept the clearing. Once sure the scene was clear, ever the detective, she scanned the area for signs to confirm what her shredded memories told her.

The ground to the right of the tent appeared dark, stained with blood, as did the large stump that stood there. The ground in front of the stump seemed sunken, as if something lay there for some time. Scuffed footprints marred the area around the depression. One area of dirt by the fire had a claw mark etched deep into the soil.

Lydia studied this mark. Ignoring the protest of the wounds on her legs, she stooped beside the now smoldering fire. By the way each line of the mark pierced the earth, she could tell it came from a rear right paw of a large carnivore—a large, hungry carnivore. She swallowed the panic and pinched her eyes closed against the memory of the beast bounding across the clearing. And a second one?

A memory flashed, another beast had pounced on her attacker.

Pivoting in place, she recognized signs of a struggle on the far side of the fire. Claw marks made by two animals had turned grass and dirt. Her heart pounded.

No sign of humans in the campsite. Someone had dressed her wounds. Although the act of bandaging wounds didn't seem threatening, something about not knowing whose hands touched her made her feel violated.

Though faint, the recollection of fingers caressing her skin became so vivid Lydia almost missed the whispered voices coming closer. She raised her weapon and, still crouched, turned toward the sound.

A couple of uniformed officers made their way through the trees. Lydia holstered her gun, and with effort, stood and walked to the edge of the clearing to greet the men who, quite obviously, came to find her.

"Ahem," she cleared her throat, struggling against the urge to yell at them to leave. She was fine and needed to investigate this more on her own.

"There you are," said the man in the lead. Sergeant Adams. He closed the distance and shook her outstretched hand. "We've been looking all over for you, detective." His voice held genuine relief.

His companion paced the perimeter of the campsite, his eyes taking in signs of the struggle. "There was concern that you were in danger," he said, eyes still darting over the ground.

Lydia shifted her stance as he prowled around the evidence of the attack. It felt as though he was judging the layout of her sock drawer.

"Why?" she faced the man she knew. "Adams, this is my vacation. What's going on?"

A nasal voice from behind asked, "Detective, were you attacked?"

"Last night an animal must have been hunting and decided that I would be easy prey." Why she couldn't give him a straight answer, she didn't know. Aside from the annoying behavior of this officer, their presence brought her a sense of security. It irritated her that the force couldn't manage twenty-four hours without her.

When the curious policeman returned to his study of her campsite, she asked Sergeant Adams, "Who is this guy? And what's going on?"

"Detective Henson. Transferred in from Monroeville." Adams lowered his voice and leaned closer to her. "He likes the uniform."

She raised an eyebrow. The uniform itched; she couldn't wait to ditch it when she made detective.

Adams shrugged. "Don't ask me." He took a breath, and the next sentence seemed to explode from him. "The Butcher's body wasn't in the house."

"What?" Of course it was, she'd delivered the head shot. She saw him go down.

Adams' gaze never left hers. "When the coroner arrived to remove the body, there was nothing there. Even in that kind of chemical fire, there would have been some identifying remains."

"Of course there were remains. He burned up. Damn it, he was collapsed and on fire when I left that house. If there's no corpse . . ." She paced away. Then turning to face him she scowled. "Who would remove it? Who could have? No one would have had the opportunity."

Now Adams cringed.

Henson stooped to glance inside her tent. "It's our impression that he walked away on his own."

Lydia stared. "That's ridiculous." She cut an angry glance at the detective. "And get out of my tent."

"Detective, I think it would be better if you got all the details from the chief." As Sergeant Adams spoke, he placed his hand on her shoulder.

Lydia flinched as fire erupted and ran the length of her arm. She wilted with agony. Both policemen reached to support her.

"The hospital should be your first stop," Henson said from behind.

Adams squinted as he looked her over. "I think he's right."

They walked Lydia to a boulder and helped her sit. "What are you doing?" she demanded when they ducked inside the tent.

"Packing," came the reply. It wasn't like she could do it, so she bit her lip while they packed her gear. She let her bare feet play with tufts of grass that sprouted around the rock.

How could the Butcher have escaped a fire, gotten past two trucks of firefighters and all the neighbors gawking at the show? Someone was wrong, must have missed something. *Jesus, must I do everything?*

The officers stacked her things on the ground and collapsed the tent. While they worked, they stepped on and scuffed traces of struggle from the night before. She'd told them an animal had attacked her, so they had no reason to keep the area pristine. Yet it took all the control she could muster to keep from shouting when Adams stepped on the claw mark she'd examined so closely a few moments earlier. He covered the fire with a bucket of dirt.

Her feet seemed fine as she gingerly slipped on socks and hiking boots. She refused to let her co-workers tie her shoes for her, so she stretched with care and slowly completed the process.

The hike back to the parking lot proceeded with uneventful slowness. Lydia used a long stick to help her navigate the terrain. At the start of their trek, she ached deep into her core. However, as they progressed, her movements became more fluid. She was relieved she didn't have to rely so heavily on her stick.

Once at the cars, Sergeant Adams told her they would take her car to the hospital. She almost insisted on going to the station first, but dismissed the idea in favor of having time to pick Adams' brain.

"What makes you think he walked out on his own?" she asked as they pulled out of the lot and onto the quiet highway, gritting her teeth at the bump.

The countryside sped past the window. She shifted in her seat. "Adams."

"Yes?" He didn't look at her. He knew she wanted details and didn't intend to tell her anything.

"Just tell me if you did a sweep of the house." They didn't just take the MT's word for it.

He cleared his throat. "One of our guys entered when the MT came up empty. CSI swept the house, but the chief wants you to go over it. We posted guards at the house till you get there. No one will tamper with the scene."

Lydia crossed her arms. Her perp escaped surrounded by cops, firemen, and a crowd of bystanders, and they thought a couple of guards would keep people out? It wasn't Adams' responsibility, it was hers. She never should have attempted a vacation.

*

One benefit of being a detective was that she received a high priority at the hospital. Because they had radioed from the car on the way, the triage nurse ushered her right into a room. After another argument, Sergeant Adams consented to return to the waiting room. Despite his concern, he was a coworker and she didn't want him trying to help her undress.

She slipped into a gown placed on the bed by the nurse who took her vitals. She noticed again how much easier she moved now. While stretching and bending to test this, the doctor knocked on the door and entered. Embarrassed by her rather compromising posture, touching her toes, Lydia straightened and climbed onto the bed.

The doctor grinned and looked at the chart in her hand. "Hi, I'm Doctor Dora Anuszkiewicz, but you can call me Dr. Dora. So, why don't you tell me what happened?"

Lydia recounted what she could about the attack. She treated it like a police report, leaving out her emotions. She also didn't mention the other animal that seemed to rescue her. That memory seemed too far–fetched to have happened. While Lydia spoke, the doctor placed the clipboard on a nearby counter and listened to her heart and lungs.

"All right, let's take a look at these wounds of yours." She eased Lydia back onto the exam table and cut away the bandages on her shoulder. "We should probably start you on an antibiotic. Being as an animal attacked you, I think a rabies vaccine as well. You don't have a fever . . . " She stared at the shoulder.

The doctor leaned in for a closer look. Lydia could feel breath on her neck. Her hand clenched to control the sudden urge to forcibly stop the doctor's breathing.

The doctor moved to look at the bandaged leg, this time cutting away the blood soaked wrappings without saying a word.

When she had the leg exposed, the doctor stood back and drew a tired hand across her face. "Detective, how long did you say you were in the woods after the attack?"

"About twelve hours. The attack happened last night."

"Did you use any ointment or cream when you bandaged these injuries?"

"I, ah, don't know. A friend did it. It was hard to pay attention. Why?" Lydia pushed onto her elbows to take a look at her leg. She gasped.

Nothing. Nothing was wrong with her leg. The skin appeared as whole and healthy as when she last showered, and showed no sign of the raw pink of a new scar, much less the oozing bloody mess she expected. With disbelief, she glanced at the pile of blood-soaked bandages next to the tray, then at her impossibly healed leg. She rubbed her thigh. No ache, no soreness.

Suspecting what she would find, she reached for her shoulder and discovered it intact as well. Moving her gaze to the doctor, she asked, "Okay, how did this happen?" It wasn't a dream, the bandages proved that.

"I don't know," the doctor admitted. "I'd like to get a sample—"

They both jumped at a knock on the door. When the doctor stepped back, Adams came into the room. "Sorry. Are you almost ready to go? Chief needs us. Now."

Lydia slid off the table and slipped on her pants under her hospital gown. "Ready." She had no intention of playing guinea pig. There had to be a logical explanation for what happened. Though, happily, she didn't have to think about it. She turned from the door and away from Adams, removed the gown, and put her shirt on. "Thank you, Doc," she said, ignoring the stunned expression on the doctor's face.

"Detective Davis," Dr. Dora said with outstretched arms, as if to stop her. Her coat flapped, and for some reason its every movement grated on Lydia's senses.

"I'll let you know if there are any other problems." Lydia walked to the door.

"You at least need to start those rabies shots. Just wait a second." Knowing the doctor probably spoke from experience, Lydia stopped and pressed her head to the doorjamb. As the doctor passed, Lydia longed to reach out and shove that irksome white coat. Thankfully, it moved on too quickly, robbing her of the chance.

Adams paced in front of the room, obviously anxious to get going. Lydia raised an eyebrow. "So you talked to the chief?"

He gave her a blank look.

"Sounded pissed?" she asked.

He let out a breath in a huff and started walking again. "Henson got back and the chief was irked that I didn't take you to him first." After a couple of circuits, he stopped. "So?"

"So . . . what?" She was anxious to leave, too, but her lips twitched upward at his agitation.

"So did they have to stitch you up? Did they give you meds? How bad is it?" He looked at her leg with concern.

"I'm fine, actually," she said in the most nonchalant tone she could muster. She couldn't begin to explain to herself how she'd healed, so she couldn't begin to explain it to someone else.

"Are you telling me you fought off a wild animal without even a scratch?"

"It's healed up well." She avoided his look of disbelief. "They said I just need to take it easy. Ya' know, no mountain climbing."

The sergeant let out another huff and continued pacing. She hid a grin by glancing down the hallway for someone to come give her the shot and release her.

Just as Sergeant Adams looked about ready to hunt someone down, a nurse arrived with a syringe and a prescription note stating when Lydia should return for the second shot in the series. The injection hurt, but she tried to ignore the pain.

"Ok, let's go." the sergeant led the way out of the hospital. Lydia kept up with his brisk pace; she couldn't wait to be out of there.

"Good grief, I thought we would never be able to leave," he said. When they got to her car they both paused at the driver–side door. "I guess you want to drive." Another pause and he handed her the keys. Of course she wanted to drive.

As she pulled out of the hospital parking lot, Adams plugged in the siren and set it on the dashboard.

Lydia did not say a word while they flew along city streets. She suspected the chief had treated him harshly for taking her to the hospital before the precinct. The chief didn't like his orders disobeyed, and as the emergency room took about two hours, they were late.

However, Adams had made the right call, and she doubted it would turn into a formal reprimand. As they neared the precinct, Lydia mulled the case. Perhaps they already had a lead.

Chapter 5

The office of the chief of police had not changed in the twenty-four hours since Lydia last stood in it. However, Chief Fairweather now showed considerably more strain. It appeared as though he hadn't slept, and she reasoned it had something to do with the fact that in the thirty seconds it took for her to walk to his office, his secretary answered the phone five times.

"You look fine," the chief bellowed when Lydia entered. "Your corpse got up and left." He grabbed papers from his desk and tossed them at her. "Horse shit. That's what it is."

She looked at the papers in her hands. The first report, an official statement from the coroner's office, revealed technicians found no human remains at the scene. The second, from the fire department, stated no casualties resulted from the fire. It's what she expected to see, so the irritation that rose startled her.

As she sifted through the pages, the chief said, "I want you to go out there and find where the hell he went. Fine–tooth comb, you hear me?"

She bristled at the insult. "I am always thorough." She dropped the reports on his desk.

"Fine. Whatever." He waved his hands dismissively. "Next time, I want you to bring him in. I don't care if he's still on fire. Cuff him and bring him in," he said leaning on his desk and staring into her eyes.

"Yes, Chief."

"Good. Get out." He sat, picked up the phone and started to dial.

She smiled slightly and left. All in all, she got off easily. If her injuries had still existed, he would have been more sympathetic. Not enough to tell her to go home, but he would have assigned Adams to go with her.

She went directly to her office and called the firehouse that had responded to the fire. No one answered, so she left a message. Hungry, she opened the top left drawer of her desk and pulled out a granola bar. Absently chewing, she grabbed her crime scene bag and headed to her car.

*

Very little remained of the house after the fire. Two-by-fours, remnants of the frame, protruded from the rubble like ribs from a carcass. The manicured lawn and flower garden that hid the sinister nature of the occupant lay trampled and muddy. Where once this house blended so nicely into the neighborhood, now it and the land around it seemed a disturbing scab on the quiet street.

She parked her car in front of the house, behind a black–and–white patrol car. The officers talked and drank coffee inside the crime scene tape, keeping out reporters or even neighborhood kids who would run into the ruins on a dare or in an attempt to find some treasure left behind.

Many times in her career, she entered a crime scene only to find evidence trampled or tampered with by the local population or reporters vying for a scoop. The yellow tape attracted more than deterred some people. Most would come as close as they could to stare at whatever carnage laid beyond. Others would get a thrill by crossing the tape. Doing something forbidden gave some people a high.

Lydia glanced around for these inevitable voyeurs. Across the street in a white ranch house, an older woman peered out a picture window from behind a curtain. Seeing Lydia, the silver-haired woman quickly ducked behind the material.

Making a mental note to interview the woman, she approached the officers. "What's up, Officer Webb?" she asked, reading his nameplate.

"Nothing, really," he replied. "A few kids in the house behind this one were daring each other to run up and touch the timbers. Smitty here came around and stood behind them." He indicated his partner. "They were scared to death when he tapped one of them on the shoulder."

She glared at the two men. Guarding the house didn't extend to playing with the neighborhood kids.

Smitty shifted his weight and chimed in. "The parents were on the back porch when I came around. They laughed harder than we did."

Trying to rein in her annoyance at the patrolmen's goofing around on the job, she took a deep breath. "Nothing else, then?"

They shook their heads.

"What about the old lady across the street? Do you know if anyone has been over to interview her?"

"Not that we're aware of," Webb said, taking a sip of his coffee. "We were just told to keep the place clear until they could get you out here. And now that you're here—"

"You stay put," she interrupted. "I don't want reporters or neighbors climbing up my back while I'm looking around." She turned her back to the affirmative noises they made and walked up the driveway to the ruins, following the path she used the night of the raid. The concrete stairs, pristine with white paint two days ago, now charred and black, cracked as she stepped on them to enter the remains.

She walked carefully through the ruined house. The smell of charred wood and melted plastic still permeated the air. In the area where the kitchen once stood, flames had burned through the floor and into a crawlspace. A gaping hole in the floor marked the place where she had last seen the Bestial Butcher as he slumped against the collapsed table.

Could he have gotten into the crawlspace? She knelt at the edge and shifted her position to lie on the floor with her head just over the threshold. Not able to see much because of charred floorboards under the linoleum, she inched further into the hole. Holding onto the edge with one hand, she reached into her belt for her Maglite, twisted the top, and looked around.

Dirt comprised the floor of the crawlspace. From where she hung, it looked sandy. He could have fallen down the hole and rolled in the sandy dirt to quench the flames. Lucky bastard. The more she attempted to peer into the dark recesses for a sign he went this way, the more certain she grew that he had.

Unfortunately, she found no proof in the sand. The water used by the fire department washed any trace of a print from the soil. The only way she would find even a partial print was by going down. How was it she always got the dirty jobs? At least it wasn't a sewer this time. She wriggled out, swung her legs around, and dropped into the hole.

Standing at her full height, her nose barely topped the blistered vinyl of the kitchen. She stooped below the floor line and glanced around. Two faint lights toward the right side of the house pierced the darkness. After looking for any other light source, she figured the Butcher must have moved in that direction. The space restriction forced her to move on hands and knees. As she slowly crawled toward the light, she examined the floor.

The water had only washed in to a point from the back of the house. Once she passed the cleaned soil, she found carcasses of dead bugs littering the path before her—spiders, millipedes, and an odd one that appeared to be a cross between a cricket and daddy-long-legs. Roaches scattered from the glow of her flashlight, lending credence to the theory that they would be the only creatures to survive an atomic blast. She moved further, trying to ignore a tickling on her leg.

Then finally, she reached a broken window and found a large disturbance in the dirt. Swirls in the soil showed the Butcher's attempt to flee the scene by squeezing through the hole in the glass. He used the mound of dirt to push his foot against as he wriggled out. Because of the sandiness of the soil, she could tell nothing from the indentation except that he truly did escape on his own, and that he used this path as his route.

But she'd seen the bullet hit. She saw him engulfed in flames. Now that she knew how he escaped, she'd love to know how he survived. *Impossible.*

She moved closer to the window, careful to avoid the few shards of glass that lay inside. Most of them littered the wilted grass on the other side. The frame of the window held prints in the ash where he apparently gripped the frame to squeeze through. No more than smudges and not one of them useable.

Frustrated, she smacked her thigh where it tickled. Turning back toward the hole in the kitchen, something caught her eye. In the wood just above the inside of the window, a tuft of hair moved as she exhaled. She reached into her pocket and pulled out a Ziploc bag. Carefully, she turned it inside out over her hand and retrieved the hair. She moved the plastic back, zipped it shut, and crammed it into her pocket.

It wasn't much, but at least she had a lead.

Her focus on the way to the window made her almost oblivious to the bugs, cobwebs, and sheer creepiness of it all. On the trip back, however, she fought for control as she knelt on crunchy bug bodies. A large rodent of some type ran across her peripheral vision to the right and snapped the last straw of her reserve. Shivering, she groaned and moved as fast as she could to the daylight shining through the kitchen floor.

She burst into the light, and after taking a glance around to be sure nobody watched, she shuddered and swiped at her hair and clothes. One of the spider-cricket things fell off her clothes. "Ugh." She shuddered again and climbed out of the opening.

In the charred remains of kitchen, she pulled the bag out of her pocket and took a closer look. Brown and knotted with hair roots attached, the tuft appeared to have ripped out when he passed the splinter. She rounded the hole to where the back door had stood. The fire had burned the rear wooden stairs to ashes. She gathered herself to jump down. A voice from the next yard made her pause. "Do you want a hand?"

Ryan Williams. What the hell was he doing here? He had not crossed the police tape, but if she issued an invitation, he would come across in a second.

"No, thanks." She jumped and landed with ease. "What are you doing here?" she demanded when she reached the tape.

In a small way, she enjoyed seeing him. She'd found the last twelve hours to be disturbing and part of her didn't want to be alone. But she'd always enjoyed her solitude, so craving the annoyance of his presence also irritated her to no end. She despised her sudden vulnerability.

"Interviewing witnesses." He grinned, his green eyes alight with mischief.

His obvious comfort irked her even more. She wanted him removed from the area, despite the fact that she enjoyed his cocky smile and wanted him to stay. *I'm going insane.* However, since no law prohibited him from gathering information from witnesses for his story, she just nodded.

"The old woman across the street saw a dark figure run from the fire just after the firemen arrived," he revealed.

"Silver hair?" she asked.

"Yup."

She bit the tip of her tongue. It wasn't his fault he interviewed the witness before she did. Frankly, the chief should have sent someone out here when he realized the body was missing.

"When I drove up, she was peering through the drapes. I thought she might have seen something," he said.

Her lips twitched. "When I drove up, too." This information, coupled with the evidence in her pocket, solidified her theory that the Butcher fled the house. "I'll be talking to her in a few minutes."

"Like that?" he asked incredulously, raking her with his sexy green gaze.

Sexy? Where the hell had that come from? Lydia crossed her arms over her chest to disguise her unease.

Ryan said, "You're a complete mess. She'd never let you in."

"Yeah, I just crawled out from under the house." She shuddered at the phantom bug crawling up her back. "I guess I should clean up first." They walked around the edge of the property, he on one side of the chain link fence and she on the other. She fought the impulse to glance at him.

When they reached the front yard, she went to Webb and Smitty who chatted against their police cruiser. They put her in mind of a comedy team, one large and tall, one thin and short. Their foolish grins made her want to laugh. She wondered how anyone expected them to stand guard when they looked about to run off and *partay.*

"We can open the site up to the owners now. I found what I was looking for. Could you run this back to the lab?" She held out the bag. "I have to get cleaned up so I can conduct some interviews."

"Sure," said Smitty, taking the bag from her. He grasped it in a way that prevented Ryan from seeing the contents. Most of the force worked with this kind of caution to reduce slips to the press.

Webb said, "So your place is cleaned up already?"

Maybe the sun had gotten to him. "What are you talking about?"

"Someone broke into your house and trashed it. They found it last night when they were looking for you."

Air caught in her throat. She wavered, as if Webb had picked up a two–by–four and knocked her in the head.

Ryan glared meaningfully at Webb.

How did he know? "When did this happen?" she asked.

"You were examining the scene." Smitty said then elbowed his partner in the side. "No wonder you can't get a woman. Classy, genius."

Breathing slowly, she asked, "Did they find any evidence of who did it?"

"No, but the rumor is, whoever it was pissed all over your clothes and bed and stuff." Finally seeing the revulsion on the other men's faces, Webb grimaced. "Ah, sorry," he stammered. "I hear they assigned Detective Henson to it, though."

"God." She raised her eyes to heaven and closed them. No wonder the new detective rode with Adams to pick her up. He wanted to get a look at the victim.

A few more deep breaths and she excused herself. Why didn't the chief tell her? Or Henson? Or Adams? Apparently everyone knew but her. Turning on her heel, she strode back to her car.

"Take that straight to the lab," she said over her shoulder.

Telling her would take her focus off the case, she realized, answering her own question. She hadn't realized the importance of her transient belongings until now. The idea that someone gained access to them without her permission rankled. That they damaged them, enraged.

"I've got what I need for my story. If you're going home, I live nearby. Mind giving me a ride?" Ryan trotted beside her.

Her initial reaction urged her to tell him *no chance in hell*; however, the growing part of her that didn't want to face seclusion won. She needed company.

"Yeah, whatever." After driving about a mile from the scene, she realized, "What about your car?"

"Caught a ride with the film crew."

"Hmm." He continued to talk about the crew, but Lydia didn't really listen as she wove in and out of traffic. What would she find at her place?

*

When they pulled into a space down from her building, Ryan said, "I live just over there," and waved toward his apartment.

"Hmm." *Like I care where you live.*

Completely preoccupied with getting home, she took off down the sidewalk. His quick steps told her he sprinted to catch up. It pleased her that he had to run.

When they arrived at her building, she punched the code to open the door and took the steps two at a time. When she got to her landing, she stopped and stared.

Crime scene tape stretched across her door. Apparently, once the police realized what had happened to her apartment, they came out to dust for prints. Black fingerprint powder still coated the outside of her door and the knob.

Ryan joined her, appearing at her side. Although his presence comforted her, a sudden burst of irritation spurred an impulse to push him down the stairs. *Where did that come from?*

"Well, let's go," she said shaking off the urge. Removing one side of the tape and letting it hang, she put her key in the lock and turned the knob. An odd odor overpowered her as she walked into the apartment. Sniffing her hand, she realized she could smell the fingerprint powder. She never realized it smelled before.

Powder dusted the entire room. That, she knew, came from the police. However, the rest of the mess held a completely foreign signature. A glance at the kitchen told her everything in the cabinets laid ruined on the floor and countertops. How dare someone enter her house without her permission? Nothing smelled right, looked right. The place she should feel safe.

She looked closely at gouges in the wall. These impressed her. "What did he do? Take a knife to my wall? Who does he think he is, Freddy–freakin'–Krueger?"

Ryan grunted at her dark humor.

Standing in the hall that led to her bedroom, she detected something that didn't smell anything like the powder. She stormed into her bedroom throwing open the door and staring at the pile of clothes and her bed.

"Who in the hell would do this shit?" she shouted. "I don't have any clothes." She waved her arms. "I'll be damned if I'm sleeping on the floor, or a bed full of piss." She glanced at Ryan. "I'm not going to bother washing them."

He followed her to the living room. "I'll just call someone and have it all taken to the dump."

She stalked toward him, pointing an accusing finger toward her bedroom. "Who would do that?"

"Do you think it could have been *him*?" he asked so softly she almost missed it.

This stopped her raging. A chill of fear ran down her spine, and she slowly looked at him. Why hadn't she made that connection? How did the Butcher know where she lived? Shit, she was in the phonebook. Frustrated with a lack of perception that was so unlike her, she growled. Lost, betrayed by her own senses, she stared at the chaos that ruled her living room.

"Look, I live across the street. If you want, you can come over and get cleaned up," Ryan offered. "I'll run out and grab a pizza or something. Bet you haven't eaten all day, have you?"

Shaking with tension, she admitted, "A granola bar this morning." She gazed down the hallway again. Then remembering the one object she cherished, she ran to the bedroom. *The pendant.*

Holding her breath, she scanned her dresser for the ornament. Frantic, she checked her bedside table. Ryan came into the room. She could tell he also held his breath while he helped her search. Then, steeling against revulsion, she started for the bed.

Just as she reached for it, he yelled a muffled, "No!"

He pulled the dresser away from the wall. She went to him as he crouched and picked up her silver pendant. She choked back a sob as he held it out. Clutching it to her chest, she allowed him to lead her out of the awful mess.

She placed the pendant in her pocket when they reached the living room. More in control, she said, "I'm feeling real grungy. I think I'll take you up on your offer."

Having nothing of value left in the apartment, she didn't bother to lock the door. As she followed Ryan's broad shoulders down the stairs, a little voice scolded her. *What are you doing going to a man's apartment?*

Shower. That's all. The scent of his cologne drifted to her and her stomach clenched. The smell both attracted and repelled her. God. *Shower, that's all.*

Chapter 6

As they took the stairs to Ryan's apartment, Lydia thought twice about accepting his offer to clean up. Not that he was a stranger. In fact, she knew more about him than she knew about most people.

When he had first appeared at her crime scene, she couldn't shake a wary suspicion and called the paper to check his credentials. When he kept appearing and giving her tips, she ran a full background check.

He came from an average family, two sisters and a younger brother. Both of his parents still lived. He graduated with honors from college with a degree in journalism. Ten years ago, he started working for a newspaper in upstate New York.

Three years ago, he went missing while doing a story about ice fishing. After he surfaced, he did a piece about surviving in the wilderness that ran nationally and almost won him an award. She read it. It wasn't bad—not preachy, like most of the survivor stories she came across.

Shortly after the article, he left the paper and wrote freelance, never staying in one place very long.

He applied for a job with the *Daily Times* as soon as he arrived in town. When he was hired for the police beat, the public devoured his columns. After he started covering the Bestial Butcher case, the papers flew off the shelves.

The rest of the report glowed as well. His credit score soared in the high seven hundreds. He never called in sick. He volunteered sporadically at the homeless shelter. And to top it off, his coworkers believed him a man of integrity and honesty. She would be hard-pressed to use the shower of a more trustworthy man.

She sighed, rounding a landing for another flight of stairs. Perhaps her nervousness stemmed from the fact that most of the dates she went on rarely ended at *his* place. Subsequently, most of those men never asked her out again.

She liked her privacy, and she liked her routine. Whenever someone came into her life, it upset the order of things. She ended up off balance and irritable. One old boyfriend actually accused her of having obsessive-compulsive disorder. What an idiot.

She reminded herself that this was not a date. He simply offered friendship. Without the experience of a real friend, she hesitated, and that disturbed her most of all.

At Ryan's apartment, she paused while he unlocked the door. Pulled from her thoughts, she scanned the hallway. The brown walls and green doors seemed like most of the other apartment buildings in the city. A baby cried in an apartment down the hall. A car drove by on the street below, blaring its radio so she could feel the bass.

Inside, his apartment held nothing particularly remarkable. No satanic artwork. It didn't reek of pot or filth. So she turned her attention to her guide, who walked to a short hall and opened a door.

"The bathroom is here. Clean towels are in the closet." He set her pack inside the bathroom, leaning it against the sink. "What do you like on your pizza?"

"We're eating?" she asked. Then when he nodded, "Anything's fine. Thank you." She appreciated his approach to an awkward situation.

"You like soda?"

"Anything diet." She really wanted a sweet vodka martini, but she only drank at home. In another venue, it could make her too vulnerable to those who would take advantage.

"Cool." He picked up his keys and went to the door. "I'll be back in a bit."

After he left, she turned and took in the apartment. Surprisingly clean and welcoming, it did not appear at all as she'd expected.

More than anything, she wanted to curl up on the couch and

sleep away the stress of her day. After running a hand through filthy hair, she thought the shower a better idea.

The bathroom sparkled as if Ryan bleached it regularly. Or had it done. In her experience, most men didn't spend time scrubbing. She dug through her pack for the clean clothes she kept in there, somewhere. Then she reached for a towel and washcloth and found them stacked neatly in the closet. She revised her idea of a maid. *This guy's a real neat freak.*

As soon as the water came to temperature, she stepped in, sighing as the warmth penetrated her hair and massaged her head. After scrubbing everything, she stood, letting the warm water run down her back, and thought about how all evidence available pointed to the fact that Ryan Williams was not a normal man.

Most men she knew did not take this much pride in their homes. She suspected most men would stay while she washed, in the hopes of getting a look as she got out of the shower.

She toweled off and enjoyed being clean again. She studied her naked reflection in the full-length mirror on the back of the bathroom door. The area that had sported bandages that morning appeared clear. No redness. Not even the light pink of a healing scar. She pushed on her neck, just above her collarbone, and felt no pain. Her body did not seem hurt at all, even though she clearly remembered sustaining the injuries.

She pulled on a T-shirt and a pair of jeans, and then moved her pack to a space by the front door. The long fibers of shag carpet cushioned her bare feet as she walked across the living room.

She needed to find a place to stay. Sitting on the couch, she reached for the phonebook on an end table. Then she made a mistake. Relaxing into the overstuffed softness, phonebook resting on her lap, the exhaustion that plagued her caught up with her, and she promptly fell asleep.

*

Ryan climbed the stairs, carrying a large supreme pizza with a six-pack of diet cola balanced on top of the box. Ordering the pizza had turned into a chore. He could not stop thinking about how the woman he wanted more than anyone stood naked in his shower.

The idea preoccupied him as he fumbled with his keys in the lock. He entered the apartment and breathed the smell of soap and shampoo. Placing his burden on a kitchen counter, and not hearing the shower, he glanced around for Lydia.

He found her in a fitful sleep on the sofa. She'd dozed off with her head tilted to the side and his phonebook on her lap. Her legs twitched slightly. The soft lips he'd fanaticized kissing curled back, exposing her teeth. An odd growling noise escaped.

He sighed, and reached out to wake her, gently shaking her shoulder.

*

Lydia ran though a park. Despite the warm humidity of the night, the breeze whisked away her perspiration as she ran. A woman ahead of her staggered while trying to tuck a twenty-dollar bill into a blaze orange bra barely concealed by a dingy green tank top. The heel of the woman's black leather knee-high boot caught in a crack in the sidewalk and she fell, ripping her fishnet stockings, and cutting her knee.

Lydia approached. The woman smelled like sex, now mingled with the scent of blood, and it fueled Lydia's hunger. She closed in. Pounced, mouth open. Ready to bite waiting flesh.

A hand on her shoulder held her back. Furious at the restraint, Lydia spun to confront the cause.

*

Lydia startled awake. Her eyes wide, she rolled off the couch, gripping Ryan's wrist.

"Hi. Sorry, but I thought you would like to eat," he said, withdrawing his hand from her grip.

"No, *I'm* sorry." She stood and tried to orient herself. "I was just having the most vivid dream."

"Oh, what about?" He sounded interested as he turned to the kitchen cabinets and pulled down glasses. "Ice?"

Still shaking off the fog from the dream, she replied, "What? No, it was odd." When he dropped two cubes into a glass and rattled it, she stammered, "Oh, sure." She sat on the edge of the couch, wide-awake now. She took her glass from his outstretched hand and took a sip, then a gulp.

They ate for a time in silence. She gazed out the window to the street below, watching but not seeing the activities of the patrons of the neighborhood bar next to the coffee shop.

"He had to pass so many people to get into my apartment," she said, playing with a piece of crust.

"So you *do* think it was him?"

"Who else could it be?" she asked. "Over the years, I've made plenty of enemies. Most of them would prefer to wait and kill me in my apartment rather than trash it and piss everywhere." Her shoulders tensed in annoyance. "Whoever did that," she said, jabbing the pizza crust toward the window, "wanted to leave a message."

"Well, that would explain the bedroom," Ryan said.

"Mmm." She bit into another slice of pizza. Swallowing, she asked, "Can I use your phone? I have to get an update on what's happening with the break-in investigation."

"Sure," he said, reaching for his bottle of water.

She dialed and left a message for Henson to call her with an update. When she hung up, she tapped the receiver thoughtfully. "Sergeant Henson came with Adams to pick me up from the campsite this morning."

"Word has it that he's new. Trying to make his career," Ryan said, grinning. "It's possible that he realized where you were and asked to tag along with Adams when he went to get you."

"Why didn't he say anything to me this morning?" she asked, wishing again for some vodka.

Ryan shrugged and reached for another slice. "Who knows? Maybe, he thought the guy that trashed your place would try to track you down. Maybe he just wanted to take a look at his competition."

She stared into her glass. "Jesus, I hate office politics. We're all on the same side. You'd figure we'd be above this bullshit." She paused, gritting her teeth to bite back a sudden flash of temper. "Well, I got attacked by something last night."

"Some-*thing*?" Ryan leaned forward now.

"Yup." Seeing his extreme interest, she held up a hand. "This is off the record, all right?"

He seemed about to drool all over himself. Perhaps she shouldn't tell him.

"Off the record." He nodded.

"I just need to talk about this to someone." Something in her gut told her he was trustworthy.

"Understood." He looked at her shaking hands. "Would you like something stronger than diet soda?"

Oh yeah, she did. Something to take the edge off. "Vodka?"

He didn't seem threatening. If he intended to rape her, he would have tried when she was naked in the shower.

Minutes later, she sipped vodka and diet cola, and then slowly told Ryan what happened the night before. "It seems like a dream now. I have no evidence of the attack, no marks, so I can't prove anything." She expected to see disbelief on his face. She only found concern. "What?" she asked.

"Nothing." Setting down his drink, he looked her in the eye. "You must realize how this sounds."

"Like I'm crazy." She downed what remained in her glass and slumped against the back of the couch. "Am I going crazy?" she half whispered.

"No," he said, smiling. "Crazy people don't ask that question."

That actually was a comforting observation. "Then what else could be wrong with me?"

He didn't answer.

Lydia didn't have an answer, either. She walked to the kitchen counter and mixed another drink. Clouds of soda billowed around ice and vodka like smoke around a fire.

"The fire!" she declared, raising her glass as if in a toast. "He was cooking meth. Those fumes are toxic. I'll bet I got a lung full, and now I'm hallucinating." She couldn't think of a more logical explanation. Proud of herself, she took a long drink.

"Wouldn't you have been high at the press conference, and yesterday when you first got to the campground, too?" He didn't look at her. Instead, he intently pulled apart a pizza crust and dropped the crumbs in the box lid.

Her elation evaporated as she realized he was right. Frustrated, she paced the length of the room.

Ryan watched her for a couple circuits, then, in a gentle voice, said, "Hey. You need some rest. Why don't you crash here for the night? I'll take the couch."

Lydia stopped, focused so much on the mystery of her experience at the campground and the unsettling dream, she'd forgotten about the need to find a hotel room. Another lapse. Her brain was turning to mush.

A glance at the digital clock on the microwave in the kitchen told her it was nearing ten. By the time she found a vacancy, got there and checked in, it would be close to midnight. Not that she could drive after the numerous cocktails, anyway.

"All right, thanks." She sat. The room spun a little as she landed. "Tomorrow I'll get a hotel room." Although she would not drive anywhere, the time had come to cut back on the drinks. She set the glass on the coffee table and glanced at Ryan.

He continued to crumble pizza crust into the box. Why was he so quiet? Her instinct said he was preoccupied with something. *He knows more than he's offering.* She wanted to question him, but with the alcohol and exhaustion clouding her brain, any attempt would appear obvious.

He still seemed lost in thought, so she took the opportunity to study him. Everything in the way he held himself showed confidence and sincerity. Nothing at all in his body language suggested anything but a perfect gentleman.

His hair fell forward a bit as he leaned over the coffee table. The shadow of a beard softened his somewhat angular features. His long fingers ended in perfectly manicured and clean fingernails that betrayed his job behind a desk.

She remembered the way his muscles flexed underneath his clothes as he moved about the apartment. They had to be well defined to announce themselves so prominently. *He must go to a gym.* The thought prompted a vision of him working out, doing shoulder presses. Warmth bloomed in her abdomen and spread throughout her body.

Suddenly, he lifted his head. The movement made her gasp for breath, unaware she held it. He smiled, revealing slight dimples she'd never noticed before. The warmth radiated into her face. Was she glowing? She frantically searched for something to say, but could not come up with anything better than, "Uh, we should be getting to bed."

Grinning now, he said, "Sure."

Realizing what she'd said, she fought the urge to cover her face in her hands. "I mean me." She took a deep breath. "I should be getting to bed. That your bedroom?" She pointed to the only door in the apartment she'd not used.

"Just let me get a fresh pillow and blankets for you." He rose and entered the bedroom. She followed and would have offered to help, but fatigue and the drink had her head spinning. He stripped and remade the bed and tossed a pillow from the closet onto it.

As he worked, he explained, "Sometimes my brother comes over when his wife kicks him out. I keep this stuff ready just in case."

"That's good of you." She crossed from the doorway to sit on the bed. "Does it happen often?"

"Depends on the time of year." He picked up the pillow and comforter he'd removed. "Around the holidays, it gets bad." He winked at her. "I don't think he'll show up tonight."

She smiled. "Well, good night."

"Night." He closed the door behind him.

She slipped out of her pants and under the soft sheets, moaning softly as her head hit the pillow. All the muscles in her body started to relax. She sensed something safe about this apartment, but nothing she could readily put her finger on. She fell asleep struggling with the thought of finding another place to stay.

Chapter 7

A soft tapping on the door woke Lydia. "Yes?" she said with a lazy stretch, comfortable in the softness of the sheets. Waking in strange places was nothing new to her. While growing up, she changed homes often enough. However, in every one of her *homes*, she had never experienced such a sense of belonging as she did here.

"It's just after eight," Ryan's voice sounded from beyond the door. "I thought you might want to get moving."

The nightmares of the past couple days returned slowly, creeping up on her consciousness like a cat stalking a mouse. "Oh!" She flung her feet over the side of the bed and pulled on her clothes. "Thanks," she called.

Her hands twitched as she glanced at the unmade bed. If he wanted to change the sheets, making the bed would make it more difficult. With no real knowledge of how he liked things done, she settled for straightening the tousled fabric and left the room.

The aroma of fresh muffins and coffee greeted her. "Oh, they're warm," she cooed, lifting a blueberry muffin to inhale the steamy aroma.

"I just got back," Ryan said, sipping his coffee. After watching her take a bite, he turned to the small television in the corner of the room. No sound emanated, and text scrolled along the bottom of the screen. She gave him a look and he explained, "I didn't want to wake you."

She yawned and picked up a packet of sugar for her coffee, dismissing the bachelor's lack of sugar bowl. Breakfast and the muted television showed thoughtfulness she hadn't expected. "Thanks." She rewarded him with a small smile that he returned.

"Ah," he motioned toward the TV. "There was an update a couple minutes ago on Officer Jacobs. They said he'd be released from the hospital this morning. I would have thought he would be off duty for more than a couple of days."

"Oh, yeah. I was told that he would be able to recuperate from home until he's healed enough. They said it could take up to a month."

Ryan turned off the mute, and the weatherman started to describe a line of showers that might skirt the area. "I sure hope they don't disrupt the tournament this weekend, Bob."

The anchor returned the banter. "We can only wait and see. Thanks, Jason."

"The tournament." She sank into the couch. "That damn golf tournament will have booked up the entire city."

An odd sense of despair settled over her. She'd been homeless before. Just after she turned sixteen and ran away from her foster family. At least this time, she had some savings. Perhaps she could rent a furnished studio for a while. But the two rents would break her. She straightened her shoulders. Hell, she'd sleep in her office if needed.

Ryan cleared his throat. "I have to get to the paper, but you can stick around and make your calls if you want." He rose and walked to the door. "Here's a spare key, just in case you need to crash here again."

She took the key. Even with the clean background check, she wondered at his motives. "You wouldn't mind?" she asked, still holding the key at arm's length.

"What man would mind having a beautiful detective stay the night in his bed?" He laughed. "All I ask is that we compare notes on the Butcher case." When she directed a fiery look his way, he raised his hands. "I'll only publish what you allow." Something told her he'd keep his word.

"If I'm here this evening, I accept your terms." She smiled. "Thank you for last night. My sleep was blessedly dreamless."

"Well, that's good," he said, glancing around as if unsure of his next move. "Okay then, I'm off." He moved swiftly to the door. "Just leave the key if you find somewhere else to stay."

Lydia closed the door behind him and breathed a sigh of relief. Grateful for a place to stay, she wondered why no residual awkwardness or unease remained between them. Even after he left abruptly. In fact, she felt quite at home. Even though nothing in the place reflected her style, she was more comfortable in the apartment of a man she barely knew than she had been in her own.

This morning, everything seemed right. She decided not to call hotels after all, a decision that made her feel more relaxed than she'd felt for as long as she could remember. Getting ready for her day, she mentally ran down her to-do list. She had interviews to conduct, test results to read, the hospital to visit for the rabies vaccination, and dinner to pick up as reciprocation for Ryan's hospitality.

The thought of that last task brought a smile to her lips, and for the first time, she looked forward to getting home at the end of the day.

*

Lydia sat in her small office and read the report on the hair she'd found. She slammed the paper on her desk. The noise halted Adams as he walked past.

"Problems?" He stuck his head around the doorjamb and smirked, and then flinched at the stare she leveled in his direction.

"Yeah, you could say that." She pushed the report toward him. Although she'd never worked with a partner in this precinct, she considered him the closest she had to it. He had accompanied her on several cases and stakeouts. They'd pulled all-nighters poring over clues, and they'd put away their share of criminals.

And although he had a reputation as quite a ladies' man, nothing developed more than a plutonic understanding. When she first started working with him, he put the moves on her as a matter of course, flashing a grin and cavalierly offering to show her the sights. After turning him down several times, he finally resigned her to the position of "one of the guys."

Now she looked across her desk at the paper Adams lifted, and growled under her breath. "Animal hair." She waved at the page. "No animal broke into those apartments. There were no tracks at any of the scenes."

"They're saying *Canis lupus* fur." Adams sat in the chair across from her, and set the paper down. "I don't remember seeing a dog at any of the scenes. Did all the officers on the raid file their reports with you?"

"Yes." She shook her head. "And none of them reported seeing anything flee the fire. Not even a rat."

"He had to leave the house somehow."

"Well, duh." She crossed her arms and leaned back in the chair.

"I am just saying," he lifted his hands in surrender, "that if he waited until the officers were gone, he would not have been seen."

She slammed her hand on her desk. "Right! A dog would not have waited; it would have run out barking its furry head off. Only a *person* would have the intelligence and the control to wait in the crawlspace of a burning house for a chance to escape unnoticed."

"What are you saying?" Adams crossed his arms and leaned back in his chair. "That the lab is wrong, or that the Bestial Butcher is a beast after all?"

Without warning, a wave of disorientation washed over her. She raised a hand to her forehead, her fingers like icicles against the ache that throbbed there. The chill gave her some relief.

Switching hands, she shook her head. "No, I don't know." She dropped her hand and contemplated Adams, the closest person she had to a relative. "This case keeps getting screwier and screwier." She ticked off points on her fingers. "We assume that his body would have gone up with the house, but it doesn't. The only possible clue left at the scene was dog fur."

"And you were attacked and your apartment was broken into," said Detective Henson, standing in the doorway, holding a folder.

"You've matched the DNA," she said, more a statement than a question. She didn't know what to make of this detective. During the day, several people stuck their heads into her office to warn her that he intended to wheedle his way onto the Butcher case.

"Yup, to your *dog*." He drawled the last word and sat in the other chair across from her desk. "I also intercepted a report regarding a hair found under Jacobs' right middle fingernail."

Replete with fury, Lydia fought the urge to jump across the desk and throttle the twerp. With effort, she schooled her features and folded her hands. "And?" Pleased that her tone didn't give her away, she found waiting for Henson to flip through the folder slightly more tolerable.

Finally, he pulled out a page and passed it across her desk. "If you look closely, you can see that the hairs you found on the scene and the one found under Jacobs' nail is the same." He waited with a hopeful look, as if expecting a pat on the head.

"And the DNA sample of the urine in my apartment matched that of the hair."

"Yes." Henson leaned across her desk. In a conspiratorial tone, he said, "Lydia, you were attacked and your apartment was trashed by the Butcher." He almost whispered the nickname.

Although she'd possessed no evidence, she'd come to the same conclusion the night before. Now she had hard evidence. Just another nail in his coffin when she caught the bastard. Was it her, or did Henson enjoy this far too much?

For the first time since Henson entered the room, Adams spoke. "All right then, what's our next move?"

"First, I have to get another rabies shot today." She grimaced. The corners of Henson's mouth twitched slightly, testing the limits of her control.

"Fun. Do you need a lift?" Adams asked.

At least no one could see the steam pouring out of her ears. "No, I need you to go question the little old lady that lives across the street from the torched house."

"Little old lady?" Adams raised an eyebrow.

"Use your charm. She's a busybody, but she could be skittish. I have a feeling she saw something." Lydia hoped so, anyway. "Perhaps she'll remember more than a shadow with the proper interviewer."

"You got it." He gave her a playful salute and left.

She turned to Henson. "Your guys went over my apartment with a fine-tooth comb yesterday, right?"

"What are you looking for?" he asked, interested.

"Clothes, shoes, anything salvageable." Not that she wanted this creep pawing through her clothes any more than a homicidal maniac.

"Anything that wasn't pissed on?" He chuckled and she felt the heat of her rage rise in her cheeks. "I think one of the gals can put together something for you. I'll have her bring it by." He walked to the door, then twisted around and smirked. "It seems to me that this *dog* is coming after you personally. Maybe you should hand over this case to someone more detached and objective? Someone who isn't a target?"

If she couldn't get this smartass out of her office soon, she would put him through a wall. Leaning forward, she quietly replied, "Being a target is an asset. When I want him, he'll come to me." She paused a moment, then continued. "And being as you solved who broke into my apartment, your interest in this case is over. I'd like that file now."

He looked at the folder in his hand, reluctantly taking the two steps to her desk, and handed it over. Chagrin radiated from him. The firm, thin line of his lips and the hardness in his eyes told Lydia he would try to find another way to insinuate himself into the case.

*

Sergeant Adams pulled his police car to the curb in front of Annette Lenz's house. He had stopped to check into her background before he ran out to question her. Heck, he didn't need an eighty-year-old woman falling apart because he made a comment about a child who hadn't called in over a month, or her husband who died last year.

But the interview should be fairly straightforward. Ms. Lenz had never married. She had worked in a clothing factory until it closed, and now she kept busy as a self-employed seamstress. Many of the women in the area had gowns altered by Ms. Lenz. In fact, she came highly recommended.

He went up the front walk, wondering how she would welcome him. In a normal investigation, he would have made this visit two nights ago. However, the police raid had caused the fire, so he doubted she witnessed any crime committed. He really needed her daily observations of the person who lived across the street, and if that person was around of the night of the fire.

Glancing at the front window, he saw the drapes move. Smiling, he mounted the steps. As he lifted his hand to ring the bell, the door opened a crack. Her security chain clacked against the wood.

Two eyes peered around the doorframe. "Yes." Her voice wavered slightly, though not from age. He sensed a trace amount of fear.

She was a full foot shorter than him and silver-haired. Her cherubic face pinched as she squinted around the door.

"Hello." He pulled his badge from his pocket. "I'm Officer Adams."

Her eyes darted from his badge to his face and back again. "If you have a moment, I would like to ask you a few questions about your neighbor." He folded his wallet and waved it over his shoulder.

"I talked to a fellow yesterday." She stepped back and closed the door enough to unhook the chain. "I didn't see too much." She motioned him inside. "Would you like something to drink?" She led him into a front sitting room, then bustled down the hallway, presumably into the kitchen, without waiting for him to accept. Much like his grandmother.

The room resembled the front room of his grandmother's house with white walls, landscape art, and antique furniture. Sofa and chairs with thin padding on ornate wood frames that looked as though they would give under any weight. He carefully sat in a chair by the window, attempting to see through the gauzy curtains.

The carcass of the burned house across the street ruined the view. He leaned back in the chair in an effort to get a better look, and his rickety perch groaned in protest. Startled, he quickly straightened and glanced around for Ms. Lenz. The sound of ice tinkling into glasses reached him.

Breathing a sigh of relief that she had not discovered his mischief, and that the chair held firm, he decided to stand.

Clasping his hands behind his back, he wandered to a credenza located opposite the entrance of the room. Multiple picture frames were arranged on top, all of which contained photos apparently taken at final fittings for dresses Ms. Lenz had altered. Prom dresses, wedding gowns, and in a few it appeared she'd sewn dresses for entire wedding parties.

"Ms. Lenz, these gowns are beautiful," he called down the hall. Nothing.

"Ms. Lenz?" Instinctively, he rested a hand on his gun and unfastened the thumb break in case he needed to draw his weapon. He moved along the hallway, fighting the urge to call out again.

When he reached an arched doorway, he could hear a scraping sound around the corner. He leaned against the wall, breathing in shallow puffs. The idea that the Butcher might not be human made him more than a little anxious.

His grandmother once told him to beware of a world beyond his perception. The last time he'd visited, she rested her bony hand on his and told him to carry a talisman with him wherever he went. She had pressed an ornament of some saint into his hand. He didn't really believe in luck, so that disk currently resided in a junk drawer in his apartment. Hell of a lot of good it did there.

The sound of a screen door falling closed came from the rear of the house. He drew his weapon, and taking a deep breath, spun into the kitchen.

His gun leveled at the only thing in the room that moved—a cat. It sauntered across a center island toward a tray that held two glasses of lemonade. Halfway across, it stopped and crouched. Leaning its head over the far side of the counter, it meowed.

Something didn't feel right. Instead of holstering his weapon, he scanned the kitchen and a dark hallway that led to the rest of the house. He moved along the wall toward that hallway, around the island and the cat.

When he cleared the counter, he found Ms. Lenz, dead. She lay on her back with her legs tucked under. Whoever killed her had allowed her to slip silently to the floor under her own weight.

He stepped closer. Her light blue eyes stared toward the ceiling. The cause of death was obvious at this angle, her throat ripped open. Blood from the injury pooled around her head and stained her silver hair a dark maroon.

The edges of his detachment frayed at the sight. By the nature of the wound, he could tell she'd died instantly. Probably without fear. Her last emotion most likely that of being startled.

Adams moved around the front of the counter to the kitchen door that faced the backyard. The heavy door stood open. Only the screen remained closed. In the dirt beyond the cement doorstep, a fresh print caught his eye. It looked like a man's hiking boot, about size eleven.

After searching the remainder of the house, he called Detective Davis. She would want to work the scene while forensics took a cast of the print.

"Davis," she answered in a strained voice.

"This is Adams. I'm at the Lenz house. You need to get over here. Now."

"I just got pumped up with rabies shots. What do you need me there for? She not talking?"

"Nope. It appears the Butcher came in and ripped her throat out just after she let me in." He suppressed guilt that he hadn't followed the old woman into the kitchen.

"What? How the hell? Shit, are you okay?"

"Yeah, he got away though." She released another string of expletives he decided to talk over. "He left a distinct print this time. I'm about to call in the lab guys, but I thought you would want to check out the scene first."

"Christ, okay. I'll be there in fifteen minutes. Call 'em in. Just let them get started. I'll be there soon."

"Got it," he said, ready to hang up.

"Hey, Adams!"

He lifted the phone back to his ear. "What?"

"If that reporter from the *Daily Times*, Ryan Williams, comes by, hold him for me, okay?"

"You got it." He nodded. He knew the reporter talked to Ms. Lenz the day before.

"Don't let him cross the police line. I just need to talk to him."

"Right." He hung up and looked around the kitchen again. The cat still sat on the counter, only now it regarded him with accusation.

"Hey, I didn't do this," he said to the cat. With a slight twist of its head, the cat walked to side of the counter, then hunched to lick its paw.

Chapter 8

Lydia drummed her fingers on the steering wheel as she whipped in and out of traffic. The bulb on her dash streaked the cars ahead of her in red. The rabies shot hadn't hurt as much as she expected; however, it still presented an unpleasant experience. The call from Adams nearly pushed her off the emotional tightrope she walked.

Growling in frustration, she waited for a minivan to edge out of her way. Ms. Lenz's murder pitched her plans for the whole evening. She intended to surprise Ryan with Chinese food from her favorite restaurant, a little bit of everything so he could pick what he liked.

She hoped he would pick *her*. Running a hand through her hair, she snorted. What the hell was wrong with her? On her way to investigate a homicide, most likely committed by an unstoppable madman, and she could not stop thinking how fantastic Ryan looked sipping his coffee that morning. Another car in the way. This time a cherry red convertible with a bleached–blonde driver babbling on her cell phone, oblivious to the siren. Lydia slammed her fist into the dashboard.

When she arrived at Ms. Lenz's house, the forensics team had already arrived and the area bustled with activity. A yellow police line fluttered in a slight breeze. The coroner's van waited at the curb with its driver lounging against the rear bumper. The front door of the house stood open, and figures inside crossed in front of the light.

She pulled behind the van and tried to gather the tattered strands of her emotions. She had not imagined her evening going this way. She closed her eyes and leaned against the black vinyl of her seat.

Chinese food and wine, with some candles maybe. He would smile, pleased that she stayed and then . . . She shivered with the pleasant thought of the potential such an evening could hold.

Calm now, she opened her eyes to the distasteful reality before her. She stepped from her car, lifted a hand in a wave to the coroner's men, and started up the driveway.

"There you are," a disgruntled voice sounded behind her. On the other side of the van, parked by the curb, sat a patrol car. Beside the car, restrained by a uniformed officer, stood a very annoyed Ryan.

Her hopes for the evening fell even further. And what she had to do next would only make things worse. She held up a finger, and started along the drive. A strangled, "What the——?" caused her to cringe.

Although several people examined the living room, most of the activity was centered in the kitchen. Lydia made her way toward the crime scene. Adams stood in the center of the room with a pad and pencil, sketching the scene. The department photographer stood near the body, taking final shots and speaking into a headset recorder as he worked, logging each shot.

He always ended with close-ups of the body. Ralph had a sensitive stomach. Since his first day on the job when he lost his lunch all over his subject, an arson victim, he never looked at the body until the end of the shoot.

Everyone knew Ralph's problem, and knew to give him an escape route to his car. There he kept a plastic-lined garbage can so he could retch in peace and not disturb the scene. The department would not tolerate such peculiarity from any other photographer. However, Ralph's crime scene photos helped to solve cases more often than not. He was the best.

Giving Ralph room to work, she moved to inspect the print outside the back door. She crouched beside a woman with short blonde hair who readied to pour plaster over the boot print.

"Susan, what can you tell me about the print?" Lydia asked the officer, as the white liquid covered the shape.

"Not too much, yet." Susan glanced at her. "It appears to be from a hiking boot, men's size eleven." She shook her head, blonde spikes of hair wriggling with the movement. "That's all until I get it back to the lab. I'll check tread patterns, weight distribution, blah-blah." She winked at Lydia and whispered conspiratorially, "Don't worry. I'll be able to tell you if a dog was wearing them."

Rolling her eyes, Lydia stood. "Yeah, thanks," she said blandly. It was only a matter of time until the rumormongers on the force got hold of a juicy tidbit like that.

The sound of running feet and a quick glimpse of Ralph's fleeing back alerted her that the body was free for her to inspect.

Inside, she walked around a counter that held a lemonade pitcher. The spatter of blood that had landed on the glass now pooled, diluted in condensation, around the pitcher and glasses.

As she rounded the counter, the victim's knees came into view first. The feet curled behind the body, consistent with crumpling to the ground. She died while she stood at the counter. One arm lay positioned beneath the body, and the other lay draped across the victim's stomach.

Some could construe such a position as resulting from a heart attack, except for the obvious trauma to the throat. No, trauma was an understatement. The throat lay open, as if on a hinge. Peering into the wound, Lydia could see the bones of Ms. Lenz's spine. Avoiding the surprised expression on Ms. Lenz's face, she crouched between the body and the refrigerator to get a better look at the edges of the wound.

The attacker had punctured the skin, then ripped away the flesh with one single motion. The coroner would give her a more detailed analysis, since he prided himself on his thoroughness. She guessed he would also love a chance to tease her about her wayward canine fugitive.

She straightened and went to Sergeant Adams. Done with the sketching, he now sat at the kitchen table and held a purring cat on his lap.

She pulled over another chair and sat. He looked terrible. His face sagged, pale and drawn, with bags under his eyes.

"It's not your fault," she said, reaching to touch the hand stroking the cat's head. The animal froze and issued a quiet hiss. Retracting her hand, she clasped it to the other on her lap. "Why don't you go over what happened for me?"

Still scratching the cat, he stared at the table and retraced his steps for her. He recounted everything, from the squeaking chair to the cat cleaning the blood from its fur.

He lifted his head and met her eyes. "It was him, you know. He was here. He's taking out any witnesses." He trembled. The cat stood on his lap and rubbed its head under his chin. "I was just in the other room. God, he could have come after me. I was right there."

Ballsy. "Apparently he doesn't think we're a threat." She needed to give Adams something to do. Dwelling on this too long would not be good for him. She would send him to the lab.

"You are," he said. The cat stared at her.

"I'm what?"

"You're a threat. He attacked *you* the other night."

"Yeah, well." She needed to deflect this line of thinking. Not just for his sake, but for hers.

Not acknowledging her weak protest, he continued. "He hunted *you* down. He didn't attack you until you were alone and vulnerable. He'll come after you again." His voice got louder. "*You* are in danger." Almost hysterical now, he stood, and the cat climbed to his shoulder, hissing and spitting at her. "You're a danger to everyone around you."

He wasn't wrong. But this wasn't the first time she'd been a target, and it wouldn't be the last. It was the first time he'd felt the urge to comment.

Fear couldn't get the better of her; she wouldn't allow it to get even a perch. A little time and hopefully Adams would regain his confidence.

A noise behind Lydia told her the shouting raised curiosity, and she suspected the forensics team stood in the doorway, watching the scene. Jeez, cops gossiped worse than a sewing circle.

She stared Adams in the eye. "Calm yourself, sergeant."

He took a shaky breath.

"Now, take the cat, go home and get some sleep." She kept her tone low and stern, but she really wanted to turn around and disburse the dumbasses in the doorway.

He nodded.

"First thing in the morning, I want you to go down to the lab and get their results. Then write your report. I want it e-mailed to me before noon. Is that understood, sergeant?"

He appeared relieved. "Yes, ma'am."

The team in the doorway quickly found other things to do as she stood to walk him out to his car.

More news crews had arrived on the scene, and their lights flooded the area. They called out for a statement. Lydia ignored them as she accompanied Adams to the cruiser.

Ryan already stood by the driver's door. Adams slipped the cat into the back seat, then rounded to the driver's side. The cat, hissing again, lunged at Ryan and hit the window as the car started to pull away.

"Odd animal." Lydia shook her head and started toward the cameras to make a statement.

Holding up a hand to silence the questions, she spoke in a voice that, although quiet, still carried to the rear of the crowd. "There has been a homicide this evening. We believe that it could be the work of the serial killer known as the Bestial Butcher. We urge the public not to travel alone if possible and to keep their doors locked at all times. We also encourage anyone with any information to call the crime line. You may remain anonymous. Thank you." Then to the reporters, "That's all at this time."

The chorus of questions began again. Some reporters practically begged for one more tidbit. She tamped down on her temper and frowned. The three big networks and a couple of the smaller ones aimed cameras in her direction. "When we have more to release, we'll hold another conference. Thank you."

The reporters retreated with their cameramen to finish their segments. She stood alone with Ryan on the driveway, almost freezing under his icy glare.

Suddenly afraid of what he would say, she spoke first. "Need a ride?"

*

He nodded, so she led him to her car. When they were safely away from prying eyes and ears, Ryan spoke. "So you can't stop to let me know the situation?"

"I didn't know the situation." She pulled from the curb onto the road.

"You gave orders for me to be kept there. I couldn't go in. I couldn't leave to interview the crowd on my own. I had to just stand there." He shifted in his seat, staring at her. "When everyone started to arrive, they were allowed to interview the neighbors. *They* were allowed to walk the perimeter of the scene, to talk to the coroner's men. What could I do?" His voice grated with frustration. "Nothing. I got to sit on the hood of a black-and-white, under guard." He faced front, steaming.

She'd suspected he wouldn't like that she passed him by, but had not counted on this level of frustration. She should have known better. The night had shifted from bad to worse.

She glanced at him a couple times. He glared out the windshield, fury radiating from him like an oven. It was contagious.

"What the hell would you have me do, Ryan?" She stopped in bumper-to-bumper freeway traffic and turned to him. His gaze stayed fixed straight ahead. "Am I supposed to tell you everything I'm about to do? Because I stayed at your house last night, I need to stop and tell you all I know before I review a crime scene?"

"Why the hell did you keep me hostage like that? Are you afraid I might find something you missed?" He scoffed.

The traffic allowed them to move a few feet. "You think I would endanger lives because of my pride? Damn it, Ryan, I've used your tips before. What the hell is wrong with you?"

"Then why did you make me wait like a chump?"

"I didn't want you to get hurt." She couldn't look at him. Flashing lights ahead told of an accident jamming traffic. She supposed they'd be stuck in the car for a while.

"How could I get hurt?" He still sounded irritated, but his tone softened.

"We're dealing with a man who should have burned to death in a fire, but didn't. Who all evidence indicates is part dog." She caught the surprised look on his face. "Yeah, that one got me, too." She stared out her window as she continued. "He can rip out someone's throat in one swipe, and do it while an officer is in the next room and doesn't hear a thing." Her gaze returned to her lap. "It doesn't matter that it was a bustling crime scene. If he wanted to take you out, he would have."

They spent the next few minutes in silence. The traffic moved only a few more feet.

"What about you?" he asked softly.

"What about me what?"

"Hasn't he proven that he wants to hurt you?"

She waved a hand dismissively. "It's my job. I have to find him. It could be a help that he's fixated on me ..." She mulled over ways to use herself as bait.

"Lydia," he whispered.

Her eyes met his, so green, dark and deep, that her breath caught in her throat.

"I don't want you to be hurt, either." He raised a hand and brushed her cheek.

She leaned toward him, still locked in his eyes. His hand slipped around the back of her neck. Its warm strength drew from her a passion so strong it frightened her. She reached for him, her hand running up his arm. She delighted in the crisp hairs under her fingertips and felt his muscles flex while he leaned close.

She started breathing again. Heavily. Panting in anticipation. As his mouth pressed hers with delicious softness, warmth flooded her. His tongue flicked, seeking entrance. Eagerly, she parted her lips in invitation.

Their tongues danced a slow waltz. Then, changing angles, she reached for him with her other hand, cupping the nape of his neck, pulling him closer. A metallic click clapped in the car as he fumbled with his seatbelt.

With him pressed to her now, her awareness ebbed. Her blood rushed in her ears. Or was it his? They breathed as one. His hand moved to the small of her back. The rest of her body ached for his touch.

Behind them, a horn blared and startled them apart. The traffic in front of them had cleared. Shaking her head to focus her vision, she drove around the accident.

Trying to concentrate on driving, she could not dismiss his hand still resting on her thigh. Smiling, she took it in her own.

"So," she said after a while. "Do you like Chinese food?"

"I love it," he replied, squeezing her fingers.

Chapter 9

Sitting across from Ryan, Lydia attempted to use her chopsticks without dropping food everywhere. She fished in her box of beef and broccoli, intent on ignoring butterflies going berserk in her stomach, and the little voice in her head whispering to forget the Chinese and finish that kiss.

"Aha." Finally spearing a small broccoli floret, she smiled and presented it to Ryan, who tilted his head quizzically.

She blushed when their eyes met then quickly averted her gaze. Trembling, she raised the vegetable to her mouth. For some reason, tonight she could feel his eyes on her while she chewed.

She swallowed and attempted to appear relaxed. Playing with her food, she forced herself to breathe.

They sat on the floor of Ryan's living room illuminated by several candles. Before them on the coffee table stood an array of boxes from the Chinese restaurant where they stopped on the way home. Also on the table rested a half-full bottle of wine and their two glasses.

She'd agreed to the wine in the hopes it would relax her. Since the kiss, which seemed like it happened weeks ago, adrenaline flowed freely through her bloodstream. Her every action more acute than in any pursuit. However, instead of focusing her attention, she lost all concentration.

During the kiss, she'd connected with him. Afterward, she tripped over her thoughts, at a loss as to how to talk to him. She'd start to say something, then close her mouth without uttering a word.

Focused on shredding the beef with her chopsticks, she tried to slow her mind that ran a mile a minute. On one hand, she needed to stay focused on the case. On the other, she wanted to vault the coffee table and start something more than a kiss.

She shut her eyes and sighed. Oh, the way he had gripped the back of her neck. Her fingertips traced the path his hand had taken.

"Tired?" His voice woke her to reality.

He lounged against the footrest of the easy chair. His hair, free from the ponytail that usually confined it, cascaded around his shoulders. His chin wore a shadow of stubble. She vaguely remembered the scratch of it on her cheek.

"Yeah, a little." What else could she say? Her lack of control embarrassed her. She refused to give in to the primal force that insisted she run her fingers into his hair. Unless he made the first move, of course.

"Maybe you should get some rest." He stood and cleared away the boxes. Her arousal turned to fury, and she stared daggers into his retreating back. How could he be so casual? Did he kiss so many women that he could fake the passion she felt from him an hour earlier?

Coming back, he stopped and studied her. "Indigestion?"

Suddenly unsure, she lowered her eyes. "Uh, yeah." When she reached for a retort, all the snappy responses deserted her like rats fleeing a sinking ship.

He left for a moment and re-entered to a ringing phone. Picking up the receiver with one hand, he tossed her a bottle of antacid with the other.

Mortified, she opened the plastic lid. It should calm the butterflies at least. She crunched the chalky tablets and struggled to focus. Her emotions flew before the four winds. Never before, even during her monthlies, had she become so erratically emotional. How irritating!

Breathing slowly, in through the nose and out through the mouth, she leaned into the fullness of Ryan's couch and tried to remember a stress relief seminar the chief forced the department to take last year. *Picture your anxiety flowing out of you with each breath,* the guru in multicolored robes at the front of the hall had told them.

They'd chuckled behind his back. Lydia never thought she would use it. She never lost control. She just didn't. She would shake her head at the inevitable, laugh at the absurd, and occasionally feel sickened by the grotesque.

Tonight, the roller coaster of her emotions bypassed it all, encountering fear, illogic, and macabre. Nothing she'd dealt with in her entire life prepared her for the past few days and what they implied. Except, perhaps, reading horror novels.

Having calmed to a reasonable level, and with the butterflies settled for the moment, she listened to Ryan's half of the conversation. And after another second, she realized she could hear the caller's side of the conversation, as well.

". . . come by for a visit. Your grandfather deserves to have you come in for his birthday!"

"I sent a card, Mom."

"He hasn't seen you in years!"

Lydia opened her left eye a crack.

"I've been a little busy," he said softly. By the expression on his face, he hoped his tone would catch on, and she'd speak softer. Lydia could have told him that wouldn't work.

"Busy!" The shout rang out of the phone with such force he flinched and held the receiver at arm's length. "Don't give me that busy baloney."

The ranting continued and Ryan, still holding the receiver far from his ear, winked at Lydia and whispered, "My mother."

She nodded.

"Do you hear me?" his mother yelled so loudly she could be in the room with them.

"I do," he replied. "Look, I'll be able to come by in about a month, okay?" The voice on the other end lowered and he grinned. "Yes, ma'am." A pause. "Yes, ma'am." A longer pause. "You got it. Hey, Mom. Look, I have a date sitting here and—" He nodded. "Thanks. Love you, too. Bye."

"She seems rather loud," Lydia teased, deciding to let the date comment slide.

"She just wants me to come for a visit."

"Yes, I heard it's been years." She laughed as he settled onto the couch beside her.

"What she doesn't realize is that I see him almost every week. I stop in for an hour or two, have a beer and talk. He hates phone calls, thinks they're too impersonal."

She laughed. "I guess he's no fan of e-mails either."

"Doesn't have a computer. Hates almost all technology. Doesn't even have a television."

"Microwave?"

"Nope." He refilled their wine glasses, finishing off the bottle.

"Please tell me he has electricity." Her neck started to unknot, and her stomach quieted further. She could kiss his grandfather for making conversation easier.

"Only because the county made him." Ryan smiled. "Nope, the only bit of technology he can appreciate is the scope for his rifle."

"He still hunts?"

"Yup. State took away his driver's license, but they let him keep his lifetime hunting license." He chuckled. "Has to hire someone to go with him to field dress the kill and hoof it out, but he still has perfect aim."

"Why doesn't your mother think you see him then?" The detective in her could not help prying.

"Because he doesn't feel the need to tell her." He wrinkled his brow in an apparent imitation of his grandfather. "Your ma don't need to know everythin', boy." They both laughed. "Besides, she lives next door to him, and if she knows when I'm over there, she'll rope me into working around the house. I'd be stuck there for a week."

Lydia rolled her eyes.

"Seriously," he said, becoming earnest. "I actually had to call out of work once."

"You could tell her you don't have the time, you know."

"Obviously you don't know my mother." Chuckling and shaking his head, he added, "You don't say 'no' to her."

She enjoyed studying his features when he talked about his family, pride and love evident in his expressive eyes.

She thought of the family she didn't have. He smiled for others, and she wanted him to have a smile for her. Biting back jealously that rose like reflux in her throat, she listened and smiled politely while he told her stories of his grandfather.

"Pop used to be in the service. Back in the Second World War, he served as a commander in both the Pacific and European arenas. He filled me in on his adventures."

Ryan revealed a notebook where he'd taken notes on the stories. "I plan on putting these together into a book for him." He ran a gentle, reverent hand over the front cover. "The best thing is that he served in Truman's honor guard while he signed the treaty with Japan."

"Wow, that's impressive," she said. "Did you ever serve in the military?"

"No," he replied. "Neither did my father." He set the notebook on the coffee table. "So, what do your parents do?"

"I've never met my parents. I was in foster care as long as I could remember." She drained her glass.

"Oh." He seemed to stumble for something to say.

"Nah, don't worry about it." The fact that she had no family never really bothered her before. The jealousy a moment ago still baffled her.

Ryan seemed at a loss for a topic of conversation, so instead of letting the night slip away into awkward silence, she brought up the case.

"We didn't really get into detail earlier about what's going on with the Butcher." She smiled, snared by the rapt, honest attention in his eyes. God, were they always that green?

He didn't seem to notice his effect on her and her momentary distraction. "I'll listen to anything you choose to tell me."

She related what happened at the Lenz house, omitting the teasing.

When she finished, Ryan nodded. "The Butcher knew Lenz saw him escape the fire."

"He had to." She tried to think for a moment, though his steady gaze distracted her to no end. "The really odd thing is, with the car out front, he had to know an officer was in the house."

"Right."

"So why didn't he attack Adams?" She rubbed her forehead, the tension returning. She wondered if he gave a good massage. *No. Focus on the discussion.* "There was nothing stopping him. With the element of surprise on his side, Adams wouldn't have stood a chance."

"Maybe it was another warning?" Ryan offered.

She considered that, then dismissed it. "All of the warnings aren't in his character. He's vicious. No, something stopped him before he could attack again."

Ryan seemed to mull this over.

She paced the room. Moving always helped her think.

"The cat?" he offered after a while.

She turned to see if he joked and caught the twinkle in his eyes and the twitch of the corner of his mouth. "A killer with dog DNA being afraid of a cat? Not likely. Anyone who watches cartoons can tell you it's the other way around. " She pressed palms to her eyes. "What I want to know is how that could be possible. How on God's green earth does a human get animal DNA? Even if his parents were into the kinky stuff, it's just not scientifically possible. Though, what attacked me sure looked like an animal."

"Well, not everything can be explained away by science."

He drew back a little when she let her palms fall to her sides so she could stare at him in consternation.

"What?" he asked. "Just ask those people who thought they saw the Virgin Mary in the water stain under that bridge." He shrugged.

"Maybe he's injecting himself with it," she countered. "Anyway, I guess that isn't the real issue, though it still bugs me. What I really need to figure out is where he could strike next. Study his motives, his moves." She bit the corner of her bottom lip.

"Maybe you should talk to the officer who was attacked and lived."

"Jacobs," she said, and considered the idea. Aside from her, only Jacobs survived an attack. Try though she might, after the initial impact of the beast, she remembered very little of the struggle or how she managed to fend him—no, *it*—off.

Fear gripped her in its fist. The pressure of it stole her breath. Panic welled up unbidden and she fought it down. No evil would control her. Certainly fear was the most insidious evil of them all.

"How was Jacobs attacked?" Ryan interrupted, once again pulling her focus to him and off her internal struggle.

She slumped into the recliner. One way to get away from the fear was to get numb. "Got anything stronger than wine?" Within minutes, vodka martini in hand and shaker nearby for refills, she recounted the events of the attack.

"I think Officer Jacobs survived because he was bait. We had the park surrounded with some officers on rooftops, some in cars. He spent the evening wandering the area with a bottle of Jack Daniels, soliciting hookers. The clothes he wore looked and smelled like a bum's. He had the foresight to wear them the entire weekend before the stakeout. Ate, slept, and most importantly, played a three-hour game of touch football in them." She smiled. He had played the part well.

"He would swig from the bottle and spill some down his front. I remember him swearing and slapping at his chest with a grimy hand. The man should work in Hollywood." She tipped her glass and drained the contents before refilling.

"He'd perfected the persona, and in most areas of downtown, he was considered part of the local populous. Even eating in the local soup kitchen.

"I watched his performance from a parked utility van. We'd been parked there for days, knowing the beast liked to hunt in that area, hoping to catch it without having to endanger Jacobs. When they sent him in, he only had to stumble around for a couple of hours until the beast took the bait.

"It came from nowhere. Even after watching the footage in slow motion, I couldn't pinpoint the exact time it entered the park. Only that it attacked Jacobs from the right and went straight for his neck.

"We thought the attacker would walk up and try to make off with him, would try to get him out of the open, that there would be some warning. Instead, it attacked without a pause.

"We all reacted at once. My team on the ground surrounded them in seconds. The snipers on the rooftops couldn't get a shot, afraid they'd hit Jacobs." She swallowed half her drink in a single gulp and shuddered.

"I jumped in and got between them. I grabbed a fist full of the Butcher's hair in my left hand and landed a punch to his face with my right. My team grabbed at him, but he spun and bolted. I yelled the order to fire, even as I pulled my own weapon and unloaded it at the Butcher.

"Motioning several officers after the beast, I turned to Jacobs. His clothes were torn in several places and he had wounds over most of his face and neck. I called in the ambulance we kept reserved in case something went wrong." She shook her head to stop the playback.

"Nothing's gone right since this bastard started up," she exclaimed with exasperation and finished her drink.

"That's when they followed him to the house?" Ryan asked.

"Right."

"Then the house burned down and he escaped."

"We lost him. *It*. We lost *it*." She swayed in the chair. "Umm . . . " She concentrated intently on setting the glass on the table beside her and wished with all her might that the table would stand still a moment. "I should get to bed now." She looked at her bare wrist. "It's late."

Ryan jumped to assist her as she overbalanced to stand and almost toppled to the carpet. "Thanks," she slurred at him. *I'm so drunk. What has gotten into me? I never do this.* "I got it from here."

"Sure ya do."

Her feeble protests did nothing to remove him from her arm as he led her into his bedroom and sat her on the bed. He gave her a critical once-over, then moved a small garbage can to the side of the bed. "Just in case."

"Oh, come on," she protested. "I'm not that far gone." *Just warm and fuzzy.* The fear had gone and was replaced by another emotion entirely.

She playfully patted his chest, avoiding his gaze and liking the hard muscle of his chest entirely too much. Feeling his heart beat under his thin shirt, she gently moved her hand to his shoulder, contours of his body playing under her fingers. She combed fingers into his hair and stretched to press her lips to his.

Their mouths met hungrily, her body on fire with anticipation. He knelt between her knees and ran his hands up her thighs. Wrapping her legs around his back, she pulled him close. She panted when he took his mouth from hers and traced a line to her neck with his warm tongue. She moaned in pleasure.

He gripped her in a wonderful bear hug while he nuzzled her neck and breathed heavily into her ear. She licked his earlobe in return and whispered huskily, "I want you. Now." She released her legs from his waist and lay on the bed, closing her eyes. She breathed, "Right now."

*

Ryan rose and gazed at her lying prone on his bed. Her hair fanned out, framing her pale features. The mounds of her breasts rose and fell under her shirt. Hard from arousal, her nipples formed erotic peaks his hands longed to explore. He'd smelled her excitement in the living room, and it had driven him crazy trying to listen and participate in their discussion. Now, the intoxicating scent came off her in waves that made his eyes cross with need.

At his dresser, he searched for the condom his brother tossed him as a joke last month, saying he needed to get laid. *The joke's on you.* He dug through three drawers before finally finding it at the bottom of his T-shirt drawer.

A red metallic package glinted in the light from the living room. He snatched it and turned to the bed in triumph. In three strides, he reached her side. Leaning in for another kiss, he found her unresponsive.

She'd fallen asleep.

Kneeling beside the bed, he rested his head on the mattress. "Damn," he whispered under his breath. "Damn, damn, damn."

He tossed the package onto the dresser as he left the room for yet another cold shower.

Chapter 10

When the alarm woke Lydia the next morning, her head throbbed with pain. It swam as she tried to sit. Groaning, she sank into the comfort of her pillow.

Thirst consumed her. She flicked her dry tongue over cracked lips. Water. She would give her right arm for a glass of it, as long as she did not have to get up. Grunting with effort, she rolled to her side in preparation to crawl into the bathroom.

On a coaster on the nightstand stood a glass of ice water. Beads of condensation pooled around the base. It must have been there for over an hour, given the temperature in the room. Ooh, even small deductions made her hair hurt.

Beside the glass rested a small saucer with several saltines and two ibuprofen. Behind the plate, a small index card leaned against the lamp. She could see the words in the faint red glow of the alarm clock.

Just in case—Ryan

"Bless you," she whispered, reaching for the glass and lifting her head just enough to sip from it. The cold water quenched the desert of her throat. As she dined, one crumb at a time, she attempted to remember her tasks for the day.

A soft knock announced Ryan. "You awake?" he asked through the cracked door.

"Yes." Her voice echoed in her ears. "Not alive, but awake."

This earned her a soft chuckle. "I don't have any coffee, so I'm making a run to The Shop. Want anything?"

"Large black coffee, please. And something for protein, doesn't matter what." She popped the pills and prayed they worked quickly. "I have cash in the front pocket of my purse. Take what you need."

He seemed to hesitate on the other side of the door. "Back in a bit." His keys clinked a moment before the front door closed.

Finally, she sat up. She hung her legs off the side of the bed and her head drooped almost to her knees. Standing on shaking legs, she walked to the bedroom door. Reaching her goal, she gripped the doorframe. The room spun crazily, and wave after wave of nausea broke over her.

When the room steadied, her nose rested against her hand on the doorjamb. Her nails caught her attention, long and even. A habitual nail biter all her life, she hadn't enjoyed nails like this since her senior year of college when she'd splurged on acrylic ones. Now her nails extended a quarter inch past the tip of her fingers and looked lovely.

Disbelief prompted her to hold the other hand next to the first and marvel. She ran her nails down her face to test them. They felt fantastic. For a moment, she wondered how they grew overnight, then dismissed it as the second thing to go right for her lately, the first being Ryan.

Her thoughts wandered to him and stayed occupied there throughout her brief shower. By the time she dressed, her strength had returned, though her stomach still clung to its queasiness. Ryan returned with coffee and an egg bagel.

"Did I have enough cash?" she asked, glancing about for her purse.

"I didn't look." He shrugged at the withering stare she gave him. "How about you get the next one?"

Satisfied with his compromise, she nodded. "Done."

"So," Ryan spoke into the silence, "do you have plans for today?"

She studied him and considered his question. She did have plans. Of course, he knew that. Either he asked because he wanted to make conversation, or he wanted an invitation to go with her.

Something inside her wanted him to come along. Having a person to talk to, to share with, warmed her. He could be angling for a story. *Not an impossibility.* Certainly he had plenty of time while she lay passed out last night to phone something in. Instinct told her he hadn't.

"We need to stop by the lab." She smiled at his raised eyebrows. "Then I want to stop in on Jacobs. He's home now, with another week until he's back on active duty."

He nodded. "Well, I'm ready whenever you are."

She stood and lifted her coffee. "Let's go."

*

The laboratory occupied a space in an older brick building behind the current police station. Thirty years ago, the building served as the police station with a large parking lot in front. When the city council decided to construct a new station, much to the relief of the crowded officers, they dug up the lot for it and included underground parking.

For months, the counsel argued on what to do with the old building. After considering all options, they allowed the department to keep it for forensics labs.

Although the building had stood since the early 1800s, the structure still seemed solid. Once inside the heavy metal door, the smell of chemicals met her. None of the offices had windows to the hall, and very few of the doors had markings. Lydia headed exactly where she needed to go, and led Ryan along the corridor.

However old the building and however claustrophobic it made her feel, she could not deny its cleanliness. Linoleum flooring glowed white from regular bleaching and waxing. In any other such hallway, the walls would have graduating grime from decades of bumps and touches. However, in this hall, the walls seemed pristine as if recently painted. Even the corners near the ceiling bore no signs of cobwebs.

She enjoyed this building. Clutter she could deal with, understanding order could exist in chaos, but nothing good could come from filth.

Opening the fourth unmarked door to the left, she led Ryan into a small office. Several file cabinets lined the far wall. An unmanned desk to the right held stacks of folders that almost buried a desk lamp and a computer.

Without pausing, they passed through the room to the left and entered another room bustling with activity. Divider walls separated the large room into sections. In each section, a team of people worked intently. Some in the back worked in suits behind draped plastic. Those makeshift clean rooms served for more sensitive analysis.

Close to the front, a woman who leaned over the shoulder of a man at a computer glanced over the divider. "Well, hello." She smiled, eyeing Ryan, and running a hand through her spiked blonde hair.

"What do you have for me, Susan?" Lydia fought the urge to rip out those seductive blue eyes.

Although Lydia had not flinched, Susan seemed to catch the tone and soberly handed Lydia a couple of printouts. "Several hairs were found at the scene. Most were cat, a couple came from the victim, but two are canine. We're running a full analysis to see if they match the hairs you found at the scene of the fire."

"They will," Lydia and Ryan whispered in unison.

Susan's eyes darted between them. "The shoe print is also odd." She tapped the man in front of her. "Show the video."

"We have video?" Lydia asked, surprised. "There were security cameras?"

"No." She pointed to the computer screen that showed a close-up of a computer-animated person walking across the screen over and over.

"This is how a normal person walks. Heel first, then rounding to the ball of the foot." She didn't wait for a reply before bending and typing something on the keyboard. The motion of the foot changed. "This is how the killer walks. The foot lands on the ball of the foot and rounds through the toes."

"You know this from the print you found?"

"Yes. The heel barely made any impression at all. This could have come from someone tiptoeing out of the scene . . ."

"You tiptoe slowly. Adams would have seen the killer," Lydia finished the thought.

"Detective," Susan said slowly. "I told you I would be able to let you know if the print was made by a dog."

"Let me stop you right there." Lydia held up a hand. "I cannot accept that an animal that looks like a person and wears hiking boots is killing in our city."

"Could be a werewolf," the man operating the computer offered softly.

Lydia rubbed her forehead and breathed deeply. "It could be just as likely that our killer did not learn the right way to walk and lives with a dog." No one brought up that no evidence of a pet dog was found at the fire scene, where they assumed the Butcher lived. No one had to.

*

A few minutes later, Lydia led the way to Ralph's office and darkroom at the end of the hallway. Located closest to the restroom, of course.

"Come on in," called a gruff voice in response to her knock.

Ralph's workspace stood in sharp contrast to the front office of the forensics lab. The pristine desk held a computer and desk lamp, both on and functioning. Ralph sat in a chair behind it. On seeing Lydia, he stood and lifted a manila folder.

"I was just about to run this over to your office." He placed it in her outstretched hand.

"I guess we saved you a trip," Ryan said.

"Nothing in there that you'd be able to use in the paper." Ralph's lips tightened into a thin line.

"Don't worry." Lydia flipped through pictures. "He's not here as a reporter."

"They're always reporters, my dear."

She chuckled a bit as she pulled out two pictures of the victim's throat. "Could you blow these up please? I need to get better detail on the edges of the wound."

He withdrew a piece of paper from a drawer in his desk and wrote the numbers of the pictures and added several notations beside them. "Not a problem." He smiled at her. "You look peaked. Are you feeling all right?"

"Fine, thanks. Send them to this address when you're done. I'm staying in a different apartment. Mine was vandalized." In truth she didn't feel well at all. Looking at the pictures made her very hungry. Nauseatingly so.

"Yes, I heard about that." He attached the page to the pictures and set it in a basket on the wall next to a door labeled *Darkroom— do not enter when red light is on.* "You take care of yourself now."

She offered him a weak smile. "I will."

In the hall, Ryan confronted her, gripping her arm gently. "You are not fine." He held up a hand to stave off further denial. "Tell me what's wrong."

She shook her head. "I'm hungry, that's all. Next time I go to the doctor, I should have my blood sugar checked." She forced a laugh.

Ryan studied her for a minute, still holding her arm. "I know this steakhouse . . . "

"You read my mind." She laid a hand over his, keeping his hold on her arm. "Lead the way."

*

After a luscious lunch of rare prime rib and salad, though Lydia only had a bite or two of lettuce, they drove to Hank Jacobs' house.

He had received a clean bill of health from the hospital, but the police shrink ordered Jacobs to take a week to recover at home before resuming his duties. As with any officer, Jacobs didn't like his forced inactivity.

Lydia received reports that he still followed the Butcher case from home, logging into the police database and requesting copies of lab reports. Although a psychiatrist visited him once a day, something compelled her to look in on him.

They pulled in front of his suburban home, and right away Lydia knew something was off, though nothing actually appeared out of the ordinary. Canary yellow siding welcomed visitors. Children's toys lay scattered about a yard filled with green grass bordered by a white picket fence.

Flowerbeds lined the front of the house and either side of three steps leading to the front door. Tulips bloomed beside azalea bushes starting to bud. Begonias grew in front of them, little pink and red blossoms lifting their faces toward the afternoon sun.

Both cars stood parked in the driveway beside the house. Nothing seemed out of the ordinary.

"It's early afternoon. The children should still be in school," Lydia observed.

"Yes." Ryan followed her up the sidewalk to the front door. "What do you think we'll find?"

"Nothing, I hope. I just want to look in on him." She stopped short of knocking and offered Ryan a crooked smile. "Just call it maternal instinct."

"You have killer instincts, not maternal ones." He smiled.

They chuckled as she pressed the glowing doorbell.

After ringing it a couple of times, Lydia started to worry. As she tensed to move around to the back of the house, the door opened a crack and the blonde head of a woman appeared around the frame.

"Yes?" The question grated from the woman as though it took all her strength.

"Hello." Lydia peered closer. "Ellen?"

"Oh, Lydia." Ellen Jacobs breathed. "It's you." She opened the door wider until she stood framed in the doorway.

This was not the Ellen Jacobs Lydia remembered, whose hair glittered like gold in the sun and whose skin, pale as milk, seemed flawless. Her quick wit and sparkling blue eyes never failed to make her the life of any party.

The woman standing before them now seemed to have little life left. Her hair clung to the sides of her head like matted straw. Bruises covered the once flawless skin, and her eyes gazed unresponsively from sunken sockets.

Though she'd been through hell the past couple of days, Lydia thought it best to hide her reaction to Ellen's visage. Instead, she continued as if Ellen answered the door cheerfully, like normal.

"I just wanted to stop in and visit with Hank."

Ellen hesitated, and Lydia swore panic briefly animated Ellen's deadened features. "Of course." She held the door wider. "Come on in."

As Lydia stepped into the house, she shot a glance over her shoulder to Ryan. Her concern echoed in his features. He nodded at her silent request for him to ready for anything. Suddenly, she regretted bringing him along. This could turn into a trap. The only reason she didn't call in backup was because the Butcher didn't take prisoners, and nothing in his profile suggested he would.

The living room held no surprises. In fact, everything about it seemed normal except, of course, for the haggard woman standing before them.

"Would you like some coffee?" Ellen offered, her head tilted, staring at a patch of light on the carpet.

"No, thanks," Lydia declined in a conversational tone. "Just came back from lunch."

"Hmm." Ellen sank into an easy chair, her eyes glazed.

"Is Hank here, Ellen?" Lydia asked, using her husband's first name.

She wanted to sit with her and ask what happened. She longed to offer a shoulder and support for a person who, although not considered a *close* friend, she would still call her friend. However, the oddness of the situation made her edgy. She glanced at Ryan who shifted his stance and looked both concerned and cautious.

"I'm right here," a gruff voice came from the hallway.

Unable to identify the voice, Lydia reached for her revolver. No sooner did she grip the handle than she recognized Jacobs.

First, she noticed the growth of his beard. The once clean-shaven face now wore a full beard at least two inches long. It covered the whole bottom portion of his face up to his cheekbones.

He prowled into the room. Never a clumsy man, he now moved smoothly, almost gracefully, to stand behind his wife's chair. She flinched when he softly rested his hand on her shoulder. This confirmed to Lydia where Ellen's wounds came from.

"What do you want?" Layers of disrespect and contempt dripped from his tone.

Lydia smiled at the officer she'd worked with and trusted to cover her back on more than one occasion. "I came to see how you were doing, Jacobs."

He nodded. "Thanks for stopping by." He lifted his hands and under the T-shirt that clung to his body muscles rippled. The skin on those arms had healed perfectly. No sign of an attack marred his flesh.

"You healed well," Lydia said, moving to the couch. Ryan followed and sat beside her.

Jacobs' eyes narrowed and he shifted forward, fingers digging deeply into the back of the chair. Poor Ellen's expressionless face screwed up in fear, her head tilting to one side.

Seeing this, Jacobs blurted, "Oh God, Ellen, go make some coffee." He smacked the chair as if starting a horse. She darted from the room, gasping as she rounded the corner. "There's been something wrong with her lately." He smiled at them coldly. "I sent the kids to her mother's for the week. Can't have them around while their mother turns psycho. Ya know?" He twirled his finger by his ear and grinned.

"Oh, yes." Ryan spoke for the first time. "Completely."

Jacobs nodded, as if agreeing with his own wisdom.

"Jacobs?" Lydia asked. "Has that shrink been by to check on you?" She watched for his reaction.

"No, he never showed." He sat and leaned back into the chair, his gaze darting to the hallway. "I didn't call 'cause I've never felt better."

A crashing of what could only come from an entire cabinet of glasses hitting the floor reverberated from the kitchen. Ryan and Lydia both half rose from their seats at the sound, eyes on Jacobs and his reaction.

"Damn woman." Jacobs stormed from the room.

"Something is very wrong with him," she whispered to Ryan. "I need to get him back to the hospital."

"How?"

"I don't know," she admitted, then straightened when Ellen came into the room with a tray, followed by Jacobs. Ellen set the tray on a coffee table, then glancing furtively at her husband, poured a cup of black coffee and lowered her face as she offered it to him.

He accepted it and waved her off. Released, she almost ran down the hallway.

Ryan poured for himself and Lydia while she asked, "So, how are you feeling?"

"I already told you, I'm fine."

"I know, but I would feel so much better if you had a checkup."

His gaze wandered toward the hallway. "Yeah, but if they don't show . . . " His beard parted and eyes flashed in a hideous grin.

"We can take you to them, Jacobs," she said, figuring she should just come out with it.

"What!" He jumped from his chair, his mug crashing against the wall. He hurled the coffee table to within an inch from her nose. "I'm fine. I'm not going anywhere." Biting off the last word, he stormed from the room.

Down the hallway, he broke through a door. A scream and then a thump. Lydia, who'd rose again when Jacobs stormed from the room, drew her weapon and started after him. Regardless of their history or how long she'd known him, she could not allow the obvious abuse of his wife to continue.

The poor woman half stumbled, half crawled from the room. Lydia stowed the gun and reached for her.

"Oh, God." Ellen's eyes rolled. Ryan sprang from the couch to offer his support. As they helped her down the porch steps, the sound of growling and splintering wood reached them. Ellen shuddered and passed out.

"I got her." Ryan scooped the comatose woman and Lydia ran ahead to open the rear door. As he slid Ellen gently into the car, Lydia jumped into the driver's seat and grabbed her radio.

"This is Davis. I need a unit at 1015 Sunshine Avenue." Even as she spoke, guilt washed over her. She should've been able to help Jacobs. "Domestic disturbance. Taking wife to the hospital. Husband is extremely violent."

"Copy that," came the dispatcher's response.

"This is Arnold," another voice boomed over the radio. "We're close, we're on the way." A pause. "That's Jacobs' house, isn't it?"

When Ryan's door closed, she backed out of the driveway and replied, "Yeah." She glanced to her right. Ryan's mouth formed a grim line and his eyes caught hers. She knew Arnold and his partner would not be enough. "Dispatch," Lydia called again. "You better up that to three units." She flipped on her siren and sped toward the hospital.

Chapter 11

Adams heard the call to respond to Jacobs' house. He sat at his desk, fighting panic that rose in his throat like bile, knuckles whitening as he gripped a maroon mug. Since the Lenz murder and the twist of fate that spared his life, he could not relax. He jumped at every noise and felt eyes boring into the back of his neck even when he knew he was alone.

His recent anxiousness worried him more than the murder. This was not the first time he'd faced danger. In fact, two years ago, a female serial killer took an unhealthy interest in him. Always he kept his composure and laughed off the stress.

But instinct told him he faced a different situation. Nothing about this case followed the natural order, and he could not seriously consider the supernatural.

He kept his expression neutral as he sipped coffee and listened to police teams attempting to subdue Jacobs.

The chief limped past Adams' desk, pausing to listen as the officers coordinated before approaching the house. The chief had ordered an open radio and voice record of the raid. Internal affairs would want to investigate one of his men losing his mind. Recording the raid could also assist should the Jacobs family file a lawsuit down the road. It was strictly a cover-your-ass move. One the chief couldn't afford to do.

When their eyes met, Adams waved to a chair. Nodding at the invitation, Fairweather sat and leaned back, stretching his legs and tenting his fingers over his middle. They sat in silence as the raid started.

"Jacobs! Police, open up!" Pounding followed.

Crackling on the radio filled the seconds the team waited. "Do it." A rhythmic thudding started.

"Battering ram," the chief commented softly. Adams nodded. "Damn shame he cracked." Adams felt the older man's critical eyes. "You still together?"

Not exactly startled by the question, the sergeant had a response ready. "Shook up, sir, but not scrambled."

The sound of wood splintering distracted them both. Shouted orders and responses of "Clear," held them riveted for several seconds. Then the voice of Sergeant Garofoli came across the line.

"Sir, there is no one inside the home. The place is trashed. The car is here, but no one's home."

The chief straightened and pressed the button to respond. "Then he's on foot. Set up a perimeter and sweep the area. He's a danger to himself and others. Find him."

Once his boss dispersed the raid team, Adams could feel Fairweather's eyes drilling into him. "Look. I've been in this job long enough to know you're shaken."

"I was in the house." Adams spoke softly. "He could have taken me out so easily."

"You were meant to call it in." He tapped a finger on the desk calendar. "If he's followed this in the media at all, he'll know Davis is the lead on this case. He's playing with her by toying with you."

Adams wanted to smack himself in the forehead. "Her apartment was a message."

"Right. That's why I'm thinking about telling the media she's off the case."

Adams let his jaw drop. "You know there'll be no living with her after that."

"Naw, she'll understand that's just for the media, to give her some space." The captain stood and leaned across the desk, putting a hand on the sergeant's shoulder. "Don't worry, kid. He didn't leave you until later. It's not like he's going to hunt you down 'cause you got away."

Though he meant to help, the chief's comment only made Adams feel worse. He rubbed the back of his neck and resolved to go straight home to his cat at the end of his shift.

*

Ryan agitatedly rubbed his hand over his face as Lydia checked Ellen into the hospital and arranged for a therapist specializing in battered women to visit on a regular basis. After tucking Ellen safely into her room, then hearing how Jacobs had escaped the raid, Lydia asked Ryan to meet her at the apartment later. "I need to stop at the office, and visit Jacobs' kids. He'll probably try to reassert his control over them."

"Just promise you'll be careful." Ryan took her hand in both of his and stepped close. Her face flushed and her eyes dilated before hardening and darting, glancing down the corridors. Loving her reaction, he brought her hand to his chest and leaned down to whisper in her ear. "I don't want anything to happen to you."

His reward came when her breath caught in her throat, and she leaned into him for a second before stepping away and withdrawing her hand. "Don't worry. I think I'll have half the force wanting to work off the clock after this."

Glancing into Ellen's room, Lydia's brow furrowed. "I wonder if the Butcher is so bloodthirsty because of a disease." She stared into space and whispered, "If it's contagious. And Jacobs caught it." Ryan questioned if she still registered him standing in front of her, until her vision refocused. "I need to ask around here before I stop at Ellen's mother's house."

He nodded slightly and reluctantly let her jog down the hall.

In the parking lot, watching the coming twilight, he decided to follow the instinctual pull to return to the Jacob's house.

Long shadows stretched across the street as he clipped his press pass to his shirt pocket and started his car.

*

Apparently, somebody had plugged any media leaks. A cop losing it made big news, yet the street in front of the home was deserted. He drove slowly past, getting a sense of the situation. Parking a block away, he sauntered along the sidewalk toward the house.

He imagined, to a casual observer, he looked relaxed, his hands in his pockets, his pace slow. Nobody could tell he saw and heard everything around him.

A baby cried in the house next door, hushed by a cooing female voice. A trio of cats sat side by side on the porch across the street. Their ears turned forward, they stared unwavering at the left corner of the one–story ranch that, until recently, held a police officer and his happy family.

Ryan paused at the end of the driveway. The sky darkened enough now that the street lamps flickered on.

He didn't have a plan for confronting Jacobs, but Ryan sensed him in the house and went around the side into the deep shadows of the back yard.

The rear door stood ajar. Although he heard only his own breathing as he moved through the kitchen toward the bedrooms, he could not mistake the presence of another. Quick glances through the first couple doors showed the children's rooms. Toys littering the floor didn't surprise him. However, the clothes and mattresses in every room had been shredded. Feathers, foam, and bits of cloth lay over all surfaces in both rooms, with smaller bits hanging in the air circling gently in the breeze of slow moving ceiling fans.

Grunting and growling came from the end of the passage. With a deep breath, Ryan turned the knob to the last bedroom. He eased the door open, bracing for an attack. The noises issuing from a shadow in the far corner stopped.

"You." A gravelly voice sounded from the massive, rising shadow.

Trying to step into the room, Ryan pushed harder against the door. Rags and foam, obvious remnants of the bed, caught against the wood and bunched behind the door. Unlike the children's rooms, this one reeked of blood, sweat, and urine.

"Hank." Ryan nodded respectfully, using Jacobs' first name to try to put him at ease. "I want to help you." He waded through the debris and shut the door behind him.

"You stole my wife," the gravely shadow accused.

"She needed a doctor, Hank." Ryan leaned casually against the doorframe, thumbs hooked in his pockets.

"She's mine, fucker!" Jacobs bounded across the room.

Ryan stepped to the right at the last minute and the lunging man dove, headfirst, into the frame. Jacobs crumpled to the floor, groaning, spittle bubbling in his throat.

"She loves you." Ryan moved from the form and the scent of decaying meat emanating from the man struggling to rise. "She's hurt." He shifted his weight at the sound of a projectile whipping through the air, and avoided a book winging by his head.

"Hank Jacobs, you've been beating your wife."

The man–beast stood and roared at him.

"I know it's not you, not who you are. You're a police officer, Hank. You can beat this. Control it."

With another roar, Jacobs started slowly toward him. Light from street lamps streaked through the window, illuminating Jacobs' face.

His hair and beard tufted in places, like he'd been pulling at it. Prominent brows shadowed wild, wide eyes that watched Ryan's every move, almost glowing when the light caught them right. His mouth gaped, rotting breath whistling past sharp teeth, and foaming drool sliding around the corners.

"Control it, Hank," Ryan said again.

The creature tilted his head and something moved in the hair. Ears that had grown larger and more pointed twisted toward Ryan, who could only hope he reached the man inside. *Got his attention, though.* Ryan continued to speak soothingly while Jacobs approached.

Jacobs stood directly in front of him now, fetid breath wafting across the short distance between them.

Ryan removed his hands from his pockets. "I think I can help you, Hank." He searched the twisted face for some sign of humanity. "Trust me. Let me help you."

Hank stared through Ryan, tilting his head slowly to one side, as if the words would somehow collide within and make sense. After a pregnant pause, his eyes focused again, and slowly, the warped face bent into a grin. Not a pleasant smile of happiness. The expression shot a cold chill down Ryan's spine.

As the lips parted, white pointy teeth ground against one another until finally, they parted and a short barking laugh emerged. "Get out of my house," Jacobs wailed. Gripping Ryan's shirtfront in a lightning move, he threw him into the door, which splintered the paneled wood on impact.

Ryan rolled to his feet, stumbling slightly over the remnants of the door. Jacobs—no not Jacobs anymore—a creature that lunged, its fingers extended like claws. Ryan stepped aside at the last second, gripped its charging back, and pushed. It sprawled head first into the shattered remains of a dresser.

"Damn." Ryan cursed his inability to get through to the once respected cop. He glanced around for something to use to defend himself. His gaze alighted on a fallen picture. A happy family smiled, surrounded by a silver frame, which seemed to glow in the faint light from the street.

Ryan ripped the side of the frame from the rest, shaking glass from the silver bar.

The creature stood with a grunt, swaying a bit and shaking its head, flecks of spit flinging from its hairy mouth.

Ryan shifted the weapon from one hand to the other and crouched. Bracing for the imminent attack, with the piece of picture frame extended, he waited for the freight train of fur.

The impact rocked Ryan to his heels. His hand vibrated with

the crunch and slide of the silver fragment into the beast's body. Roaring filled Ryan's ears then went silent. The body of what was once Hank Jacobs slipped from his arms to the floor, a surprised expression across its now bare face.

Standing there, shaking with adrenaline, Ryan peered closer at the man. The frame piece protruded from Officer Hank Jacobs' chest. Yes, he had transformed back. All signs of the animal had gone, leaving a peaceful–looking man in his mid–thirties, face relaxed as if in sleep.

He took a piece of shredded cloth from the floor to wipe away prints from the silver frame. A cold voice within him told him nothing else could have been done. And yet, as he walked from the house into the night, he silently mourned for the life he'd had to end and for the family forever changed by a horror they would never understand.

*

Realizing she knew more medical examiners than physicians in this hospital, Lydia wandered to a nurses' station for directions to the infectious disease specialist. The haggard–looking nurses did not notice her, and understanding working long hours in a thankless job, she tried to wait patiently. She leaned on the counter and tented her fingers, resting her chin on the tips.

The three women wore scrubs in bright colors. The one closest to her had yellow covered in cartoon characters in what seemed an attempt at a cheerful appearance, marred only slightly by the residue of a brownish substance streaked like a sash across her front. This one left the station and walked down the hall without so much as a glance in Lydia's direction.

A deep breath and five seconds with her eyes shut allowed Lydia to keep her composure. She cleared her throat.

Finally, a nurse with short black hair, wearing blaring bright pink scrubs, turned and leveled weary eyes at her. "Yes?"

"I'd like to speak to a doctor who specializes in infectious disease. Can you please give me a room number?" Lydia held up her badge and ID for the nurse's inspection. "I realize you're busy tonight, but I'd appreciate your help."

The nurse nodded at the badge, shuffled a couple more files, whispered something to the nurse in aqua scrubs, and motioned Lydia to follow.

"Detective Davis." Lydia offered a hand while they rode to the third floor.

"Annalyn Murry. Sorry if I seemed short. Things have been hopping tonight." At Lydia's nod, she seemed to want to say more. "Actually, I needed to step away for a sec." A smile lit her exhausted features. "I may get to use the bathroom on the way back."

"Five minutes to breathe can feel like a two-week vacation," Lydia replied from experience. "Even if they are spent in a quiet bathroom."

The nurse led the way off the elevator. "That's the truth." Annalyn showed her down a hallway, then opened a door and stuck her head in. "Dr. Sutton?" After a mumbled reply, the nurse pushed the door wider and motioned Lydia to enter.

"Enjoy your vacation," Lydia said by way of a thank-you, and received a grin in return.

A glass wall sectioned the office. In front, the doctor displayed all the trappings of a successful physician. Large wooden desk, probably mahogany. Diplomas and certificates matted and framed. And of course, the doctor himself, a man in his mid–forties. He had brown eyes and hair, save for a silvering at the temples, and skin the color of milk chocolate. His rich, deep voice, despite his standing and extending a hand, belied aggravation at being disturbed. "Yes?"

"Sorry to disturb you, doctor." When he remained standing, she pursed her lips and sat anyway. "I only have a few questions pertaining to a case I'm working."

"Yes, I know the case you're working. I watched your interview the other day." He sat and folded fingers across his stomach. "Ask your questions."

Attempting to ignore the urge to smack the arrogant expression off his face, she spoke directly. "Is there a disease, infection of some kind, transmitted through a bite or wound that can cause irrational behavior in humans?"

"You mean aside from the obvious, rabies?"

"My understanding of the virus is limited, but I thought a person with rabies could only live for a couple weeks without treatment once they've been infected."

"Ah, no, that's a common misconception. A person can live anywhere from weeks to years without developing symptoms, however, once symptoms start most people die within ten days."

"People have survived it, though." Lydia fisted her hands together on her lap.

"Yes, most have severe brain damage. One person recently lived and is doing well after being put into an induced coma. It's a fascinating case really. A fifteen–year–old—"

"Dr. Sutton," Lydia interrupted. "In this instance, the suspect, who I believe is the initial carrier, has not had medical treatment and has been what you would call symptomatic for at least six months."

"Ah, then rabies would be a long shot." He glanced up as a woman in a lab coat slid aside the door in the glass partition and tugged a mask off her nose and mouth.

"Doctor, the sample is ready for you to view."

"Ah, yes. Thank you." He looked to Lydia. "Well, detective, do you have any further questions?"

"A few."

"Then you can talk to me while I review my results." He handed her a mask, then tied on his own. "We received a cadaver this morning whose bowel exploded, and the coroner doing the autopsy found a growth that needed further analysis."

They walked into Dr Sutton's lab where the low temperature made goose bumps form on her arms. The body lay naked on an autopsy table, open for inspection, but the doctor walked to a lab station and reviewed a report on the screen.

"You needed the entire body?" She approached the corpse and peeked inside. Most of the organs had been removed, and those in the chest were reinserted while the lower half remained empty.

"Clues can be found anywhere." He studied the screen. "Your other questions, detective?"

"Yes." She inhaled sharply. Staring into the cavity, she wanted to touch the emptiness and had, in fact, reached a finger toward the body.

Misinterpreting her gasp, the assistant apologized, "The smell is distracting. I have a cream here." She handed a tube to Lydia. "Just spread it on your upper lip."

"Thank you." She held the tube until the assistant walked away, then set it on a counter. The smell didn't bother her. Something about it seemed rather alluring.

She shook her head to clear it. Where had that come from?

Just question the doctor and get out of here.

"What about a disease that can change DNA? Perhaps disguise it to appear like that of an animal?"

"Nothing can do that aside from deliberate engineering, of course."

"Of course." She stood over the cadaver again. Her pulse raced, her breath came in shallow gasps, and she struggled to swallow the excess saliva pooling around her tongue.

"Detective?" Arms pulled her from the table. "Detective, are you all right?" Dr. Sutton stared into her eyes and snapped his fingers.

"Yes." She cleared her throat. "Yes, of course. Sorry, I must have gotten dizzy. I think I'm done for now." She reached to shake his hand. "May I contact you if I have further questions?"

Still appearing concerned, he nodded. "Sure." He caught his assistant's eye over his shoulder. "Please give the detective my card."

"Get something to eat in the cafeteria before you leave," the assistant advised as she walked Lydia to the hall.

Chapter 12

After running out of the hospital to her car, Lydia rested against the smooth surface. What was going on with her? What was up with that body? And what the hell possessed her to lean in like that? She shuddered at her behavior.

Tilting her head back against the car, she stared at the night sky. Light pollution of the city blocked all but the brightest stars. The red star, Betelgeuse, glinted and winked hypnotically.

It put her at the campsite, staring at the fire when the creature lunged from the bushes.

She screamed and crouched beside her vehicle, her gun finding its way into her hand. Panting, she scanned around. Parking lot.

"Holy shit. What's wrong with me?" she asked into the night.

"You should watch your language, young lady." An elderly woman carefully picked her way between a gap in the cars.

"Sorry." Embarrassed, Lydia holstered her weapon and climbed into her sedan. "I'm just tired," she muttered to herself.

When she backed out of the parking space, she tried to focus on getting to Ryan's apartment, pulling those fantastic smelling covers over her face and slipping into oblivion.

Actually, she still should run by her office and file a report on what happened at the Jacobs' house. But then, she would enjoy it more if she wrote from her laptop with a glass of wine in her hand while curled on Ryan's couch. She passed the turn for the precinct.

For so long, she'd never found it possible to call a place home. She'd lived in her apartment for years and could never shake the feeling of eminent departure. No collections, not many personal items, no attachments, because she never knew when she'd leave.

Ryan's apartment was different. The mismatched furniture and shag carpet comforted, as if the apartment wrapped her in an aura of safety and warmth. She smiled over that for a minute.

Then her mind wandered to the scene at the hospital. What had she thought when she leaned over the body? Succulent. Appetizing. It smelled so heavenly. She ran her left hand through her hair.

"Oh God, I wanted to rub my hair in it." A retching noise escaped her throat.

She'd experienced filthy situations before, and on several occasions, been covered in blood from wound spatter. She'd wrestled suspects in alleys where all matter of foul things found their way into her hair. But never before had she considered putting them there on purpose.

"Oh, that's just gross." She shuddered.

Flexing her fingers on the steering wheel, she glimpsed her nails. They extended a good quarter inch longer than before, and the tips appeared as white as a French manicure.

Bile rose again. *Oh, this isn't right.*

What if she'd caught it? She grew more convinced than ever her serial killer attacked to spread a disease. The doctor confirmed nothing existed that fit this description. Of course, that didn't mean all possible diseases were known. Maybe something from the rainforest, something that got away from a government lab.

Scenes of *The Stand* flashed in her mind. Not all that likely. And the movie had it right, the military would swarm if something got away from them. Homeland Security would have caught wind of the case and forced her off it weeks ago.

The highway she traveled stretched into the darkness. Headlights only illuminated a small patch of asphalt. This stretch of road cut through the last bit of nature left in the city—a wildlife preserve.

Not much wildlife lived there. The only residents seemed to be squirrels, raccoons, and rabbits. Deer or other larger animals would have to traverse much of the city to live in the preserve.

Suddenly, a squirrel darted into the pool of headlights and froze. Slamming the horn and jerking the wheel, she barely avoided the petrified animal. The right front tire caught the road's soft shoulder and skidded. She spun the wheel the other way and immediately started to fishtail. In vain, she pumped the break, tugging the steering wheel one way, then the other.

For a second, she thought she recovered control, but both passenger side tires caught gravel, and the car went onto two wheels. She screamed. The gravel under the tires gave way, slamming the car to the ground and bouncing her head hard against the ceiling. She gripped the door handle while the car slid down an embankment.

She fought for breath as the car crashed into one tree after another. The airbag deployed. The car spun like a top, and finally came to a rest with the hood burrowed into a tree trunk.

Moments lasted hours after the world stopped whirling. Lydia lay against the deflated airbag. The white powder packed with the bag to prevent rotting settled lightly on her cheek. She blinked, and groaning with effort, tried to sit up.

As all nerves reported injury, pain like fire filled her senses. She gasped and managed to lean back. Panting with anguish and unable to wrap her mind around what just happened, she stared dully out the windshield at the bark of the tree. The word *oak* floated from the depths of her memory.

She registered a faint movement to her left. She snapped her head around at the crack of a twig and the rustle of leaves. Something came closer.

Moving as quickly as she dared, she unbuckled her seatbelt and drew her weapon. She thought perhaps someone witnessed her go off the road, and maybe came to help. Or maybe the Butcher readied to finish her off.

At a thud on the hood, she aimed her gun over the steering wheel. It took her a millisecond to recognize the cause of the noise. A squirrel munched his acorn and watched her with black beady eyes. She saw the little critter clearly. Moonlight? Glancing out her window at the canopy of branches above. The moon sent its illumination through the leaves. Magical.

A crunch of acorn broke her trance.

Instead of relaxing at the obvious lack of threat, her temper flared. *Son of a bitch runs me off the road, then stops to laugh at me while he eats dinner. Well, I'll wipe that smug look off his face.* She tried to open the door. Stuck. Thumping at it with her full weight didn't budge it an inch.

Her flurry of movement startled her audience, and stuffing the nut fully into his cheek, he jumped off the hood.

"No!" she roared. He wouldn't get away.

She broke through the windshield with the butt of her gun and crawled out onto the hood. Out of the car, she read the terrain. The full moon illuminated, even under the forest canopy, better than sunlight.

Pain. Her stomach clenched and churned, and she slipped to the ground. Landing hard, she tried to stand, but pain shot through her head. Crying out, she dropped to her knees. She gripped her abdomen and howled.

Agony ripped through her entire body in waves, from her toes that screamed as if ripping from her feet, to her face and head that felt pummeled by hammers from the inside. Every inch of her skin crawled, itching, aching.

Slowly, the excruciation subsided. She lay on a carpet of leaves. Her eyes closed tightly, she panted for breath. She whimpered and tried to sit. Once free from the residual twinges, she stood hunched, gasping for air, and glanced around.

Colors popped. Oranges, reds, and greens seemed to have an electric glow. Their radiance energized her. Excited her. She scanned the area. Several yards in from where she crouched, the squirrel froze again, its head tilted, its ears perked.

Lightening fast, she leapt. In a few short bounds, she landed on the small creature, digging her nails into its stupid furry body.

Her mind roared, "Fucking squirrel! Ruin my car. Could have fuckin' killed me!" She didn't notice as she shredded the mass in her hands in feral rage.

Good. She held the fragmented guts in her right hand, and what was left of the small, muscled haunch in her left.

Hungry. She bit into the meat and shuddered with pleasure as juices ran down her chin.

Small. Not satisfying. She grunted, and searched for more. Absently rubbing the contents of her right hand into her hair, she loped after another rustle in the leaves.

*

Lydia stretched under the comforter. The perfect temperature of the sheets made her want to roll over and go back to sleep. Memories of dreams, where she ran through the woods after small animals, flitted through her mind, then faded. Her entire body lay limber and relaxed, like she spent the night having great sex. Even the room smelled wonderful. Perfumed.

With a smile, she sighed deeply. She pulled the pillow closer around her head. So comfortable. But she had to start her day.

She needed the results of the raid, and to check on Ellen and question her kids. Lydia still suspected a disease responsible for the drastic changes in Jacobs' behavior and mutation of DNA. She'd try to get through to the Centers for Disease Control today. Perhaps they knew more.

Finally ready to lift her head, she pushed to a sitting position and leaned a hand behind her. It squished into something.

"What the—"

Red coated her nails, as shiny as new polish, and dripped from her raised hand to her pillow. The dots mesmerized her, made her eyes cross and vision swim. The dots formed shapes—small animals darting through piles of leaves.

"No," she whispered. "No. It's not real."

Standing, she spun to stare at the bed. Bits of fur, skins, and unidentifiable sludge littered the comforter. Panting, her heart racing, she crouched, extending her hands over the ruin that had surrounded her all night.

"No," she said again, as if the denial could make the foul sight disappear. "Oh, no."

Her first instinct told her to gather all evidence and toss it in the dumpster. She paced the room, racking her brain for alternatives. Finding none, she stuck with her initial impulse and gathered the comforter, sheets, and pillowcase into a ball around the furry, fetid remains.

On the way to the door, she caught her reflection. Her hair stood at all angles, pasted in place as if by a red styling gel. Bile rose in her throat. Streaks of dirt and blood colored her face, arms, and clothes. Shaking, she glanced at the window, then the clock.

Five–fifteen in the morning. Ryan still slept. Maybe she could squeeze around the corner and into the bathroom without waking him. Grabbing a change of clothes, she opened the door a crack. Deep breathing came from the direction of the couch, so she decided to go for it.

The shower tested the limits of her cop sensibilities. Under the water, the gelatinous muck spiking her hair thinned and ran red down her body. Although she wanted to move quickly, she shampooed, lathered with soap, and rinsed from head to toe three times until the water ran clear and her fingers met no obstruction when she ran them through the strands.

Under the pelting spray she tried to recall exactly where she had collected the squirrels. She remembered the woods, the freedom, and the rage. A chill crawled up her spine in spite of the hot water.

The car. She braced her hands against the wall and remembered running off the road. Traces of fury attempted to rise within her. Instead of overtaking her, they made her ill. She stood until every trace washed away and she felt steady again.

She dressed and snuck into the bedroom to retrieve the macabre bundle, checking the mattress for any sign the sludge had filtered through the sheets. Dry. Well at least she didn't have to replace the mattress before Ryan awoke.

She couldn't entertain the idea that the violent dreams and oppressive hunger actually happened. For the first time in her life, she deliberately ignored what the detective in her observed plain as day.

As she moved out of the bedroom with her bundle, she remained mindful of Ryan on the couch. *How wonderful he is*, she thought as she carried the evidence of her excursion to the front door. Setting the bundle in the hall, she turned and studied his face as he slept.

He lay on his back. His hair, released from the low ponytail, framed his chiseled face. The effect tugged at her. If not for her urgent need to rid the apartment of the soiled bedding, she would close the distance and kiss those full lips.

Struggling with sudden longing, she sighed, taking a step toward the sleeping man that only a week ago annoyed her like a cloud of buzzing gnats. She turned for the exit and bumped into a small table by the door, knocking off a lamp.

Eyes wide, she snatched it out of the air. Marveling at her reflexes, she replaced it with a smile.

"Nice catch."

She spun, startled. "I'm . . . uh . . . taking out the garbage." *Sure, right.*

Rising on an elbow, he smiled. "You forgot the bag." His eyes sparkled, igniting a heat within her. Her mouth dried and her breath caught in her throat.

"Right." She stepped into the open doorway and grabbed the bag. "Dumpster out back then? Good. Okay." And without waiting for a response, she ducked out, closing the door behind her and leaning against it.

"He *has* to think I'm crazy now," she mumbled.

Then she hefted the bag of sheets in her free hand and headed for the elevator, muttering a prayer to get to the dumpster unseen.

Chapter 13

Having deposited her cargo in the dumpster, Lydia sighed. *Well, that's done.* The robin's-egg sky was speckled with cotton ball clouds and tinged with pink and purple from the rising sun. Despite sounds of the city filtering into the alley, the morning was peaceful. She took a moment to gather her nerves, her head back and her eyes closed.

You've got it, too. The thought came unbidden. She shook her head in denial and rubbed her eyes.

No. She pushed the answer through her mind.

You killed all those innocent animals.

No.

You gutted them and rolled in their entrails.

"No." She backed to the brick wall, rubbing her arms. "It was a dream," she whispered, trying to forget her bloody shower. "I've been having such crazy dreams since—"

Since you were attacked in the woods? The thought seemed to sneer. *Where are your wounds? Your scars?*

She crumpled into a ball against the wall. She recognized the voice. The voice she used when she and Adams did "good cop, bad cop." Bad cop was hers. Usually it didn't take much of her attitude before a criminal or witness spilled to the baby-faced Adams with his sensitive smile.

Bad cop whispered in the corners of her mind, forcing her to see what she longed to deny. No one could cut her a deal, make her feel safe against the harsh reality thrown in her face.

You're going to become just like Jacobs.

Her hands shook and her breath rattled in her throat as she glared at the dumpster, solid and green, holding the horrors she committed last night. "Maybe I already have."

"Have what?"

So wrapped in her thoughts, Lydia hadn't heard Ryan approach.

He wore a white T-shirt and ripped shorts. Leaning a well-muscled shoulder against the building's rear doorframe, he contemplated her.

"Shit." She jumped to her feet. "Why are you sneaking up on me?"

Holding her fiery gaze, he lifted a pizza box, and from where he stood, tossed it like a Frisbee into the open dumpster. "You missed dinner last night."

"Yeah." She brushed palms across her pants. "Late night."

He didn't move aside when she tried to squeeze past into the building. Instead, he leaned against her, pushing her into the frame.

She ignited everywhere their bodies met. She struggled to breathe, not because he flattened her, but because it was the last treatment she expected. The treatment she most wanted.

As if reading her mind, he crushed her mouth with his. Hungry with need, she wanted him to take her, and gripped the back of his head to pull him closer.

His hands tightened on her shoulders, then pressed and groped down her body, leaving a tingling trail in their wake.

His mouth left hers, nipping and licking its way to her throat. She wanted to let him continue, but his hot breath grazing the flesh of her throat left her vulnerable. Tilting her chin, denying him access, she brought her hands between them and pushed.

"I have to get ready for my shift." She headed to the apartment. Without looking, she could tell he remained in the doorway.

She fought the urge to return to him and finish the kiss. If she really caught what Jacobs had, she would turn against Ryan next.

Time to move out, she decided. Even with her mind made up, stepping into the elevator, she silently wished Ryan would chase after her, push her against the wall and take what she denied him.

She managed to put new sheets on the bed and have coffee made before she found him draped across the sofa, staring at her.

Either she'd been too absorbed in conflicting emotions to hear him, or he moved as silently as a cat. *Must be the former.*

"What?" With steaming mug in hand, she attempted to keep simmering desire from her voice.

He shrugged and lifted the remote, shifting his gaze to the television.

Closing her eyes, she stifled a sigh and finished off her coffee. Even though his attention seemed rooted to the television, something told her he still focused on her.

"Got to get over to the office today," she said while fixing another cup of coffee. "Find out what happened with the raid last night." Hopefully, she could borrow a car at the precinct. She glanced at him. "Check in at the hospital." She paused, waiting for a comment.

Nothing.

"So have you heard from your source lately?"

At this direct question, he answered, "Nope." He continued to click the remote.

Heat crept into her cheeks. "If you hear anything, call my cell," she snapped.

Receiving a grunt as response, she slammed her mug on the counter. "I'll be out of your hair by tonight."

She had no reason to be so infuriated with him, and she couldn't put her finger on what angered her so much. Once she entered the bedroom and started to stuff clothes in her pack, the anger dissipated. *I'm a fool.*

She stared around the room and realized how little she had with her. In the few short days living there, she'd become attached. Accustomed. Comfortable. More welcome in Ryan's apartment than in the one she'd called home for the last two years.

Tears stung her eyes. She'd also gotten weepier in the past few days. Furious with herself, she squared her shoulders and hefted her sack. She needed to get control. Fear that she might hurt Ryan choked worse than the tears.

Leaving she could do. She spent most of her life leaving people she'd started to care about. This was no different.

Then why did her heart rend in two? How, in only a couple of days, had she come to rely on him so much? Not to take care of her, hold her, or cushion her, but simply for his presence.

Sucking in her cartwheeling emotions, she went cold, as she had so often against the horrors and heartbreak of her job. She turned.

Ryan stood in the doorway, blocking her path. "Where are you going?"

He refused to budge as she attempted to storm past. Thwarted, she stood nose to nose with him and silently demanded he move.

His soft gaze raked over her, and though she kept her expression stony, she couldn't hold on to the flash of rage that filled her a moment before, and she allowed him to remove the pack from her shoulder.

"Lydia," he said his voice a husky whisper.

Her defenses crumbled and she fell into his arms, which wrapped around her tight and strong. She rested her cheek against his shoulder. So right, so wonderful. No tears came this time. She just breathed the scent of him.

"I think I may have what Jacobs has." She tried to lean back and look at him.

Giving her a squeeze, he released her slightly. He didn't care. He didn't fear her.

"What if I came after you? What if I hurt you?"

Lifting a finger to brush the hair out of her face, he said, "I can take care of myself."

His eyes met hers. The green of them intensified and held her, like a fly in amber. Hands, warm and firm, moved up her spine to bring her close. He slowly leaned into her. Heart racing, she licked her lips in anticipation of his mouth. This time, he came gently, holding for a moment before deepening the kiss. Heat rose between them, and she twined fingers into his hair.

Her cell phone rang. Sagging slightly, she pressed her forehead against his and gave a bitter chuckle before moving to answer it.

Although he relinquished most of her, his hand sought one of hers even as her other reached for the phone.

"Hey," Adams said cheerfully. "Wanted to give you an update."

"Go." She moved to the couch and Ryan moved with her, cupping her hand in both of his.

"Okay, short version. Jacobs returned to his place last night and lost it. While he made a mess, he managed to impale himself on a picture frame. It appears he trashed the house and fell into a pile of debris."

"Shit," she said with a sigh. "At least he didn't hurt anyone else."

"That's not all. When Ellen discovered what happened, she checked herself out of the hospital, picked up her kids, and took off."

"Why is she running now? She stayed in that house, living in fear for days." Out of the corner of her eye she could see Ryan bow his head.

"She told a nurse someone had been lurking around the house just after Jacobs was attacked. Maybe she was afraid he would come back now that Jacobs was gone."

"All right, go to the house and poke around. Take someone with you. I don't want any of us working alone." She couldn't blame Ellen for running, and she didn't know what to think about a second threat. Shaking her head she closed her eyes, one thing at a time.

"Right," he answered.

"I have a couple of leads to work on. Meet me at Lester's Diner on Sloan Street for lunch to compare notes."

"Working alone?" he asked, concern in his voice.

She smiled at Ryan brushing a thumb across the top of her wrist. "No. I'm letting the reporter tag along." This earned a mock bow and mouthed thanks.

"Ah, okay. See you at lunch." He hung up.

She flipped the phone closed with one hand. "You don't know me—" she started to say until Ryan raised a hand.

"You're wrong. I know that you're a dedicated cop. Your personal life is almost nonexistent. You have few friends and little or no family. You are harder on yourself than you should be. You're passionate." He traced a finger along her cheek and tucked a stray hair behind her ear. "And you're beautiful."

She struggled not to lean in for the promise of an ardent kiss that would lead to rolling, hot and sweaty, across the floor. "Are you sure you want to deal with this?" Her mind strayed to how she awoke. The memory snuffed the spark of passion. She wondered if she should tell him about that morning. "It could be dangerous."

"I already said I can handle myself." He shifted on the couch. Again with that infuriating half smile.

She knew so little about him, but she believed his assertion. With a nod, she withdrew her hand from his and stood.

"Okay then, let's get down to business." From her pack, she withdrew a pad and pen. Tapping one on the other, she paced the room. "We have a killer with animal instincts, and as it happens, DNA." She grimaced. "That still doesn't make sense. Maybe he's trained a dog to attack on command."

She completed one circuit in silence, then continued. "He trashes my apartment when I get close to him. He attacks Jacobs when *he* gets too close. Or had the dog attack. We have no witnesses to the attack, but even a trained dog would have made noise and Adams would have heard. Regardless of the evidence, it could not have been a dog." She slowed and stood directly in front of Ryan. "Where were you getting your tips?"

"What tips?"

"You know what I mean. I need to know your source."

His eyes climbed to meet hers. "Oh, you do?" He raised an eyebrow. She scowled. *And all he does is smile.*

"You know we don't divulge our sources." He raised a hand to halt her scathing response. "I won't. What I *will* tell you is he has been otherwise occupied and hasn't been able to get in contact. When I get something, detective, you will."

Not the answer she wanted to hear. She kicked the couch and continued her path around the living room.

"I have to act as though this is contagious. Everything points to it. Madness. Worse than rabies." She shuddered, the idea of her own contamination chilling her. "I should contact the CDC, but I want another chance to capture this bastard, first." *And I don't want to end up a guinea pig.* What a dreadful thought.

"I heard you wanted us to follow up on a lead before lunch." Ryan sat back. "So where are we going?"

Returned to reality by his question, she considered for a moment. With her idea of following up with the Jacobs family thwarted by their departure, she decided a closer look at Jacobs' body would prove the best course of action. The coroner might still be working on him.

"Coroner's office." She paused then grinned. "You get to drive."

"Goody." He rolled his eyes and picked up his keys. "To what do I owe this honor?"

She grabbed her purse on the way out. "I had a little car trouble last night."

*

As they traveled the white polished halls to the morgue, Lydia filled Ryan in on the history. "When the new station was built, they included a coroner's office in the basement. Easy deliveries, close to the labs for evidence analysis. Smaller towns use hospital morgues."

"Makes sense." Ryan nodded.

Pleased he actually listened, she grinned. She loved serving on the force in a town small enough that the crime tended toward minor infractions, but large enough to afford some of the better gadgets.

The entrance to the morgue offered nothing more than a largely empty area with a desk to one side. Across from them, a set of swinging doors waited with windows set in the top half. Lydia walked to one and peered in.

"They're working on him now." She tapped and waved soberly. "Come on." She led the way through the door and accepted a smock, gloves, and mask from the assistant.

Jacobs lay naked on his back with the Y–incision already made, flaps of his hairy chest folded to show his chest cavity. His face appeared peaceful, a drastic contrast to his torso.

Ali Hoodam, the coroner, set a rib spreader aside and moved to shake their hands. "You'll get a copy of my full report, of course. Somehow, though, I knew you'd darken my doorstep."

"Anything to tell me so far?" She avoided looking into the chest cavity and watched with amusement as Hoodam demonstrated to Ryan how to use cream for the smell.

Setting the jar aside, he stood on the opposite side of the table. "Cause of death is quite obviously the metal rod that pierced his heart through the right ventricle. A piece of a silver picture frame, sent to evidence for fingerprinting.

"Additionally, some other odd things I don't remember from the man when he was alive. It appears as though his fingernails became very thick." He held up the left hand. "Over a millimeter."

"One point three seven millimeters," the assistant amended, glancing up from a monitor.

"Yes. Usually thick nails darken or yellow. This is from either poor circulation or fungus. As you can see, these are pristine."

"They seem pointed," Ryan observed from behind Lydia.

"Yes." Hoodam extended the index finger. "To get this effect, most people need to use a file. The way the nail is curved, almost rolled into a point, suggests it could be natural, but I've seen nothing like it." His large brown eyes opened wider in amazement.

"You said *things*," Lydia prompted.

"Quite right, detective." He swept a hand over Jacobs' torso. "You've seen him at the precinct picnic at the lake. He barely had three chest hairs."

"Yeah, Monroe named them last year." She smiled over her shoulder to Ryan. "Larry, Moe, and Curly."

He arched an eyebrow at the furry body. "Looks like the Stooges hired a lot of extras for this episode."

"Doubtless," Hoodam agreed. "And he shed." At this, the assistant lifted a large, clear bag holding what looked like the clothes Jacobs wore the night before. Lining the bottom of the bag, brown hair piled an inch thick.

"Anything else?" She swallowed, stomach churning at the sight of all that hair.

"Only this." The coroner pulled back Jacobs' lips to reveal pointed and apparently elongated teeth.

"Filed?" she asked, though somehow she suspected not. His teeth had seemed normal yesterday. Jeez, just yesterday.

"No file marks could be found, and dental x–rays are not normal procedure when we know the identity of the body. Do you wish to order one?" At the shake of her head, he grunted. "We'll know more once we've scanned and weighed the internal organs." He lifted the rib spreader.

"Thanks, doc." She moved with Ryan to the door where they removed the protective gear. "Keep me posted."

*

Relaying the events to Adams at the diner didn't take long. Neither did his report of the house.

"It was a mess," Adams said after their waitress brought their orders. "I almost tripped twice, and I was moving slow. All evidence says he barged through the house. I can see him falling into a broken bit of something." He bit into his burger. "Hell, broken bits of things were everywhere," he finished around the mouthful.

"Real elegant." Lydia tossed napkins in his direction and poked at her salad. She wanted a burger, rare, but the fake ferns set about the tables put her in mind of the night before. So she ordered salad. What a mistake.

Swallowing enough to free one side of his mouth, and blotting his lips, he continued. "Cordoned off the area and took prints. The only whole prints we recovered were from the family. No signs of forced entry." Finally freeing his mouth, he sipped his cola. "Looks like he did this to himself."

She mulled this over. From the edge of her vision, she noticed Ryan staring, so she speared a cherry tomato. It exploded in her mouth while she considered their next steps.

"First order of business is still to take down the Butcher." The tomato rekindled her hunger and she started to eat in earnest. Following her lead, they finished lunch in relative silence.

When she finished, she stared at her water glass. Condensation beaded and trickled down the side. A bit of pulp detached from the lemon wedge on the side and floated, darting on eddies around the ice like a fish.

"Bait." She looked each man in the eye. "What we did before worked. It brought him into the open. We do it again. This time I'm the bait."

"No!" both men said at once. Several customers and the waitress glanced in their direction.

"Catching this bastard is my job. I'll do my job," she said, her voice calm as she lifted the dessert menu. "I hear their apple pie is very good."

Chapter 14

"Over the last three months, twenty-two bodies have been attributed to the Butcher," she called to Ryan through the bathroom door. "Fifteen of those were hookers or college girls cruising the bar scene. The other seven were homeless men. We set Jacobs up as a homeless man in the park." She paused to apply lipstick.

"And we know how that turned out," came Ryan's reply.

Before they had left the diner, they reviewed strategy and layout of the team on rooftops and as other bar hoppers. After lunch, she shopped for an appropriate outfit. Ryan escorted her into the shops, and apparently enjoyed choosing the skimpiest outfits he could find. With a grin, he had repeatedly asked her to model them. She finally selected something appropriate without his help and headed to the checkout, laughing when he groaned with disappointment.

Once in the apartment, she showered and dressed. All components were black, even the thong she slid into. The black skirt hung two inches below the curve of her rear. A bustier gave her breasts a lift and exposed luscious cleavage, and ended across her midriff showing off her tight abs.

Makeup and hair presented no problem. She leaned over the sink and gave herself a shake to make sure the girls didn't fall out of their holster. Black knee-high boots completed the look. She had only finishing touches left.

Earrings, cheap and sparkly. Bangle bracelets, cheap, and according to the women in the store, back in style. Finally, a knife in a boot sheath, and a gun in a small handbag. The handbag contained only the gun, making it easy to reach if—no, *when*—the Butcher attacked.

"All right." She exited the bathroom. "Let's go."

Ryan, who insisted on escorting her, stood ready at the picture window and gazed out over the nightlife of the street.

He looked amazing dressed in a dark blue T-shirt, jeans, and brown boots. Simple enough, but the body they encased made all the difference. Hard muscle rippled under his shirt as he turned.

Oh, God. She didn't realize she panted until she tried to lick her lips and found her mouth dry.

"Nice outfit." He motioned for her to pivot, and in the rotation, she gained some composure. That was, until she faced him again.

Only inches from him, she could smell his cologne. *Oh, my God.* She raised her hands to his chest in an attempt to keep a distance between them. Under her fingertips, his upper body rippled as he reached for her, his hands slipping around the bare skin at her waist, then over the leather covering her ass, and pulled her to him.

"Oh, damn." She surrendered and circled her arms around his neck, pulling his mouth to hers.

Intoxicated by the scent and taste of him, she executed a spin and pressed him against the living room wall. She ground her body against his, pulling at his shirt so she could rub her hands across his bare chest. Hair tickled her fingertips and she traced a trail to the lip of his jeans and fumbled with his belt.

His hand caressed her body, across the mounds of her breasts, down her flat stomach and to her thigh. She moaned as moisture built between her legs.

Her sight clouded as his finger slipped easily past the thong and into her folds. His other hand scooped a breast from the bustier and his head lowered to the tip. His tongue flicked lightly over the nipple. It hardened. Tilting her head back, another moan escaped.

A knock sounded at the door.

Finally, she got his belt undone and rubbed a hand on the prominent bulge in his jeans before moving to free it.

The knock sounded again. Louder. "Hey! Aren't you ready yet?" Adams called through the door.

They broke apart, reluctantly. Growls of frustration rumbled in both their throats.

Ryan regained composure to yell, "In a minute." The thudding on the door silenced, and Ryan gripped her by the arms. In a voice thick with need, he said, "To be continued."

When he released her, she stood for a moment, stunned. He'd not handled her that way before. She liked it. Then she stepped into the bathroom to straighten her clothes.

Though hard to shake the arousal, she left the bathroom with a clear head. All cop.

*

However, her composure nearly fell as she sat next to Ryan in the rented car. Adams drove, and Milton, the head of the city's sharpshooter division, occupied the front passenger seat. She found the distraction of the man beside her nearly overwhelming. Only by digging her nails behind her ear could she concentrate on discussions of the plan for the evening.

She'd start at one side of the club district and move from bar to bar, appearing more intoxicated as time passed.

"You can act, right?" Adams barbed over his shoulder.

"I act like I like *you*." She turned to Ryan. "The idea is for him to come after me. Keep watch on the time. Your only job is to signal me to move on. Other than that, keep your distance. Once he shows, no matter what happens, stay out of it."

"Yes, sir," he said, his voice low and husky.

Her fingers twitched slightly, aching to touch him again. She almost missed a look exchanged by the two in the front.

"Problem?"

Milton turned to meet her eye while Adams shook his head.

"Are you sure it's wise to take a civilian on so important a sting?" He grimaced at Ryan. "No offense."

Ryan smiled. "None taken."

Lydia sighed. "I need someone on the floor, and he doesn't give off the cop vibe. He's signed the waiver. He's participating."

Adams pulled the car to the first club, Bottoms Up. She and Ryan got out. With the line wrapped around to the alley, she walked to the large bouncer. *The man could be a linebacker.*

Flashing the hulk a smile, she ran a hand through her hair, knowing the jiggle it caused to her outfit. That's all it took. The bouncer offered a sloppy grin and stood aside as if she'd said, "Open sesame." She took Ryan's hand and squeezed past into the thudding, smoky atmosphere.

"Nice move," Ryan shouted into her ear.

"Not a problem." She released him and waggled her fingers in farewell as she wriggled into the dancing crowd.

After thirty minutes and several dancing partners, another man came behind her, grinding to the rhythm of the music. Even without looking, she sensed it was Ryan. She closed her eyes and leaned into him. He turned her around and the rest of the club faded. They finished the dance, then left the club.

Cool air refreshed her. She strode ahead of him to appear alone, vulnerable. Through the next few clubs, the rhythm seemed the same. After about half an hour, Ryan emerged from the crowd to dance with her and they left, using the crowd to space them apart so they didn't appear together.

Well after midnight, her frustration started to wear on her. The thumping music that stirred her blood at the start of the night now irritated her. She tried to smile and dance, but she forced it. Convinced anyone watching could tell she'd had enough, she approached a bar at the far side of the room.

Many women danced on the bars in this club. The bartenders encouraged it and rewarded them with free shots. This made them wilder, and many seemed to hold onto the poles more for stability than sensual effect.

Lydia wanted a drink, but knew it would cloud her wits and result in a penalty for drinking on the job. She ordered a diet cola and barely retrieved it before a dancer in a long, white body stocking and high heels kicked it.

"You're too serious." Ryan seemed to materialize out of nowhere.

She shrugged. He leaned over as if to shout something in her ear, but instead, he nibbled her lobe. Electricity coursed through the whole side of her body. Not enough to completely arouse her, but enough to energize her again.

"Better?" he asked, winking.

Laughing, she rose to leave. The nibble worked better than a B12 shot. Her mind cleared instantly. They had to go outside. The crowds started to thin, and she needed to get into place for attack. Almost to the door, she glanced over her shoulder. Ryan didn't follow.

At the bar, White Body Suit had fallen. Into Ryan's arms! He smiled, setting her on the floor. The voluptuous woman gripped him.

Bitch! Lydia's breath came quickly. How could he? Who did she think she was?

Lydia's face grew hot with rage. Pushing aside people, she stormed to the bar. Her vision tunneled to the blonde woman pressed against Ryan.

My man. My man.

She reached them and grabbed White Body Suit by the hair. In a flash, Ryan caught Lydia by the wrist, so she only managed a slight tug instead of yanking the bimbo to the ground like she wanted. She snarled, releasing the blonde. The woman recognized her peril and clamored to the end of the bar. Lydia smiled. Fear was good.

Still holding on to both of her wrists, Ryan said, "Time to go," and led her from the club. Once in the fresh air, he pulled her around the edge of the building. "Breathe," he commanded.

Panting, she stepped toward him. "You're mine." She bared her teeth and tried to bite his fantastic face.

"I know." He met her eyes and stared.

Her heart fluttered like he'd reached inside. Like he touched her soul.

She sensed the attack coming from the alley's deep shadows before anyone appeared. Ryan's features set in deadly seriousness, and they turned as one to meet the foe. Bounding out of the darkness, the animal roared as it burst between them, pushing them apart.

It darted across the street and into the alley on the other side. No shots fired. Where the hell was everyone? Sleeping?

She gave chase, reaching into her bag and letting it drop when her hand wrapped around her gun. Behind her, she recognized the sounds of her force organizing a pursuit.

The Butcher raced around the end of the building to the right and through another alley to the left, weaving in and out with ease. She kept pace, pausing only seconds at corners to confirm the direction her quarry fled.

Not again. She would not let him get away again. As they ran, his path appeared to be illuminated in front of her. She didn't have to listen anymore. She could see the way he went. Left. Right. Over the fence. The scent of stale sweat and dried blood led her through the city.

It seemed as though the chase lasted hours. Exhausted, yet spurred on by anger, she followed relentlessly. He led her to a large concrete wall that she scaled with ease. Landing on the other side, she paused.

They'd entered the zoo. The trail crossed a moat into the bear habitat. She prowled the perimeter. Nothing. She leapt the moat and inspected the entire area. Sticking her head into a cave, she encountered something. By the scent, she could tell it was not her prey. A growl from the pile of fur indicated she woke sleeping bears.

A small voice in her head screamed for her to run. But the raging roar she released into the cave drowned that voice. The bears silenced.

She left their habitat and searched for the trail. The cacophony of scents overwhelmed her, and she realized she lost him for a third time. She screamed in frustration, overturning a trashcan and bench.

Delicious odors rose from the spilled contents. Suddenly ravenous, she bent over the spilled can and snatched a half eaten hotdog. Chewing with delight, she tilted her head at the sound of pounding hooves.

Antelope behind a protective fence ran from her, their haunches bunched seductively. Everything else forgotten, she easily climbed into the plains habitat and stalked the herd.

Several young fell behind the adults. She circled to cut them off from the rest. Lydia howled and yipped. The more noise she made, the more frightened they became. Delicious fear. Eyes rolling, they gathered together at one corner of the fence. She stalked toward them, gauging the distance, then pounced, bringing the nearest one to the ground.

*

She opened her eyes to darkness. Strong, musky odor filled the space and a large furry body warmed her. Struggling into a sitting position, she examined last night's bed. She'd slept in the bear cave. Remnants of the antelope lay scattered in the corner. Her hosts barely stirred as she backed out.

How could this happen again? She remembered the antelope, hunting it, feeding on its fear. Shaking, she groped for her gun and couldn't find it. Shit.

Outside the cave, the zoo still lay in darkness with dawn on the horizon.

She gave herself a once-over and sighed. "Well, thank God I'm still dressed."

"You're getting neater at eating, too."

Startled, she spun.

"Good thing I have your gun." Ryan offered it to her.

"What?" She took the piece, checked the safety, and stuck it in the waist of her skirt. "Where did you come from?"

"Let's talk about that later." He took her arm. "How 'bout we get out of here now." The last was not a question as he led her to the wall she'd scaled so easily a couple hours before, and helped her over.

His car, parked a short distance away, was a welcome sight. She started to ache everywhere.

"Where is everyone?" she asked once in the car and on their way.

"Everyone was stunned when he pushed past us."

"I told them to be on the lookout. He moves fast. That's how we lost Jacobs." Though it started strong, her voice choked at the end of her statement.

He glanced her way. "They're canvassing the city, looking for you. They figure you either caught him, or you're dead."

"How did you—?"

"You need to call them." He handed her his cell phone.

"I don't know what to say." Flashes of dining with the bears surfaced in her memory, and she shook.

"Hey." He yanked her out of the memory. "Tell them you chased him into a storm drain."

She nodded and started to dial. Why did he help her? Why wasn't he scared? He should be terrified. If the situation were reversed, and she observed him crawling out of the bear cave, she would have kept her gun pointed at him until help arrived.

Adams answered. "Talk to me."

"I'm fine," she replied.

"Jesus, Davis! You ran after him and disappeared. We even got the traffic helicopter out with a spotlight trying to find you."

"Chased him into a storm drain." She conferenced in the chief and organized a sweep of the drain system. She'd never gone into a storm drain, but it made sense he could hide down there.

The captain's voice grumbled in her ear. "How sure are you he's down there?"

Asked directly, she couldn't flat out lie. "Not very. But sir, we're running out of leads."

"Even with the entire public utilities department, we wouldn't have the manpower to sweep the system."

She sank into the seat.

"I will post patrols for the next couple days. Davis, if we don't get this guy this week, I'm calling in the feds."

"Understood, sir." She closed the phone and slammed her head against the seat.

"Where to?" Ryan asked.

"Home." She warily looked him over. "We need to talk."

Chapter 15

They rode in silence the rest of the way home. Aside from an occasional glance in his direction, Lydia stared out the window. Ryan appeared to concentrate on driving. Fine, she needed time to think anyway.

Something was drastically wrong with her. What woman didn't have mood swings? But, this had a different quality. Losing control on a regular basis was unacceptable.

She started last night with wanting to rip off Ryan's clothes, nearly removed that woman's head, and then the vicious murder of that poor antelope. She closed her eyes. *Waking with the bears was just weird.*

She could have the same disease as Jacobs, and perhaps even the Butcher, but it appeared to manifest differently in different people. Small comfort. Now she had no idea what she would eventually become.

Her profession made her no stranger to violence. Few people came quietly, so now and then she needed to use force to bring them in. Plenty of times she longed to get excessive with someone particularly aggressive, so the urge for violence didn't bother her.

For years she'd practiced control. Even monthly women's issues rarely caused her to behave testily. Not to say she didn't become irritated. She just made sure she kept her cool.

Unfortunately now, every emotion seemed amplified. Anger. Passion. Oh God, passion. She'd been all over Ryan last night. He went along with it, though. But what guy wouldn't when a woman dressed like her pulled his clothes off? He seemed to want more than a roll in the sack. At least, she hoped so.

She worked so hard to maintain command of her life, to have

order. Since the Butcher started his spree, her world had spun out of control.

She needed answers and sensed the calm man beside her knew more than he offered. What had he said when she stumbled from the cave? She'd been so foggy at the time, it hadn't registered. Something about eating. What were the exact words? She pleaded with her memory.

She continued to rack her brain until they parked, then it hit her as his voice sounded in her mind. *Getting neater at eating, too.*

She said nothing until safely inside his apartment. At the door, Lydia stood in front of him, hands on hips and refusing to let him pass. "You know more about this than you're letting on."

Unflustered, he leaned left, then right, looking for an escape. Not finding one, he smiled and stepped forward, kissing her. The smell of him mingled with smoke from the clubs and another deep earthy scent she couldn't place. Strong hands slid around her waist, hugging her to him. The cool, rough skin of his fingers made her tremble. Her tongue met his and her resolve started to melt. Then he lifted her and switched their places in one fluid motion.

"What the hell!" she cried.

He marched into the hall. "Bathroom," came his muffled reply from behind the already closed door.

"Son of a bitch," she growled. Furious he'd gotten past; she promised he wouldn't do it again. She paced the living room until he returned.

*

In the bathroom, Ryan sat on the closed toilet. What the hell could he do? Would she accept what he needed to tell her? Could she come to terms with what they'd become? He rubbed the stubble on his chin. *Well, it's her problem, really.*

He only needed to tell her the truth. Lay it out. What she did with that knowledge was her business.

Plucking at a towel hanging across from him, he realized he couldn't just let her go. He wanted involvement with this, with her. She could walk out on him once she knew. He'd be surprised if she didn't.

He wanted to help her catch this guy. But then what? He had fanaticized about her, never thinking how she would react when the truth came out. He hadn't anticipated how well she'd work with him. They made a great team.

Maybe when she understood . . . maybe he had a chance. He shifted from hope to despair and back again. He didn't just want her. He needed her.

At the mirror, he stared at his reflection. Stalling. Wishing he could think of a way to do this easily. Saying it flat out wouldn't work. Quick, like a Band-Aid, didn't apply.

It really didn't matter. She would have fear and anger, regardless of the approach he used. And as much as he wanted to protect her, she deserved the truth. The whole truth. So he'd start at the beginning.

He opened the door and found Lydia, hands on hips and foot tapping. Damn, she resembled his mother waiting for an explanation.

He allowed a wry smile to curve his lips. "Yes?"

Her eyes narrowed further and she poked a finger into his chest. "Talk. Now." How did she expect him to concentrate on conversation when she stood in his face that way? Her delightful pheromones overpowered all traces of the night before. Sexy, flushed, and smelling so good.

"Fine." He waved in the direction of the living room. "Care to sit?"

She hesitated a second. He could tell she didn't trust him. He hadn't earned her distrust. Except for the kiss a minute ago. But he knew she liked it, so she couldn't be that mad.

He sat on the couch and propped his feet on the coffee table. She waited until he settled to perch on the edge of the recliner.

"All right." He fought to appear casual. He hadn't told anyone this story. "Several years ago, I was a sports writer."

"This has nothing to do with my investigation!" She stood and appeared ready to lunge at him.

"You want the story from the beginning," he spoke softly. His father taught him people would listen harder if he spoke softly, and his father was the most intimidating man Ryan had ever known. "Don't you?"

Plainly unaware of her own frustrated growl, she resumed her balance on the chair. Ryan smiled and continued his narrative.

Her appealing show of thigh caught and held his attention. He averted his gaze to the bare wall so he could think. "As a sports writer, I got to travel all over to cover games, training camps, and the like. A couple times a year, the paper would pay for me to experience some of the more extreme or remote sports."

When he glanced in her direction, she rolled her eyes, huffed, and scooted deeper into the chair. Ignoring her attitude, he allowed his eyes to wander back to the wall.

"On one trip, about three years ago, I went ice fishing. We were dropped off by helicopter at the start of the day, and supposed to be picked up eight hours later. Just me and three other guys. One of them was our guide, Martin. Good guy. Been a guide for twenty years. I couldn't wait to interview him.

"Then there was Ed, a banker. It was his second trip. He told me his wife just loved the spa at the hotel, and since she would be there all day, he needed something to do with his time. 'Man time,' he called it.

"Then there was Ugh." He paused, recalling his first look at the man who changed his life.

"Ugh?" came her disbelieving tone from the recliner.

"I never learned his name, and he grunted in response to every question. So I called him Ugh." He shrugged. "After a few questions, I gave up and concentrated on my other companions.

"We landed, drilled our holes, and waited for a bite." He laughed. "I was so excited when I caught my first and only fish. Once I got it off the hook, it dove right back into the hole.

"Anyway." He waved off the memory. "In the late afternoon, a storm started to come through. Martin put up a shelter, and we all went inside to get out of the wind. Ugh didn't come with us. He didn't say why, ya know, he just grunted and waved.

"We passed around Ed's canteen of whisky, and after a while, I needed to stretch my legs. And well, get rid of some whisky." He glanced at her again.

She seemed mildly interested.

It's a start. "I moved around the lee side of the shelter to do what I needed to do. When I came back around, I looked for Ugh. I couldn't see him anywhere. Thought he may have gotten blown into one of the holes."

Lydia scoffed.

"Hey, the wind was blowing really hard and I was half tanked. All I could think of was to get help.

"Martin and Ed came out, and we cautiously walked to Ugh's ice hole. His gear lay strewn about by the wind, his pole broken. No sign he'd taken any of his gear at all.

"It didn't sit right with the others, either. Martin told us people put up a struggle during animal attacks, but there were no signs of an animal. We blamed the messed gear on the wind. Ed thought Ugh might have fallen and reached for his pole, then snapped it.

"Martin brought the canteen out and toasted the hole. We figured Ugh fell in.

"Ed crossed himself and knelt next it. He leaned forward, trying to see something in the water. Then we heard a loud growl behind us.

"I spun around in time for a hairy shoulder to plow into me. Ed shouted and fell into the opening. Martin let out a yelp as the animal tackled him, ripping at his face."

Ryan took a deep breath and rubbed his face. "Shit, I need a drink. Want one?" He walked to the counter and poured a couple glasses of wine without waiting for her response. If she didn't need one now, she'd need it soon.

She didn't reach when he offered her the glass, just stared at him. Shrugging, he placed it near her on the coffee table.

After a large swallow, warmth filled his chest. "The creature tore into Martin's throat. Blood spurted everywhere. I couldn't move. I just watched while it grunted and Martin's blood covered the ice.

"Then Ed surfaced, calling for help. I could barely make out his glove at the edge. Suddenly I could move again, like I was broken from this horrific hypnosis. I stumbled to the edge, trying to keep my eye on the animal at the same time.

"I grasped Ed's hand and pulled, stomping into the ice for traction. Slowly, I was able to pull Ed from the water. His clothes froze almost instantly in the wind. He dropped to his knees, coughing loud and hard.

"I told him to hush and tried to lead him back to the shelter and the flare gun in Martin's pack. I thought maybe the fire would scare the thing off until the helicopter could arrive."

Ryan shook his head and closed his eyes. Damn, this was hard. He didn't want to remember. In the years since, he'd learned to cope, to live his life so he didn't have to go back to that place on the ice. But Lydia needed to know, so he took another deep breath and continued.

"The coughing caught the beast's attention. It whipped around and lunged at us. Ed screamed as the monster sank its teeth into his arm. I wasn't about to play tug of war with that thing, so I let go of Ed and ran for the shelter.

"I could hear his screams as I dug frantically for the flare gun. It took everything I had not to throw up, and all I could think was I'd left him to die."

Lydia leaned forward. "You were trying to save him," she said, her voice soft and full of sympathy.

His heart did back flips at her tone. "I tried," he agreed. "All I could think was 'flare gun, flare gun.' Finally, I saw it. And a box of flares. I got it loaded and peeked out of the shelter.

"Ed's screams actually gurgled now. He wept and begged, lying on his back with the creature standing over him."

"I aimed, and as if by a miracle, the wind died and clouds parted, giving me a good look. The creature stood upright, its entire body covered in fur except for its face and long clawed feet. It stood on Ed's shoulder. Its dog–like snout gripped Ed's arm, pulling higher like it wanted to cause as much pain as it could before ripping it off."

"*Dog*–like?" She jumped up again. "Just when the hell were you planning on telling me this?" Waving one hand as she spoke, she held the other to her forehead.

She's so beautiful when she's agitated, Ryan thought. "I'm telling you now, *detective*." He hoped using her title would help her calm. It didn't. He endured a lurch that had nothing to do with reliving the worst time in his life.

She paced for a minute or two, and he enjoyed the way her body moved, hips swaying and breasts jiggling with each step. She hadn't changed out of the clothes she'd worn to the club, and aside from a few smudges, she looked as delectable as she did when she pinned him to the wall last night. The few rips in the blouse and skirt offered glimpses of pale skin underneath. He itched to explore what lay beneath the cloth.

When she seemed to work herself into a frenzy, he asked, "Would you care to hear the rest?"

"Tell me." She continued to pace.

"Sit."

"I'll stand."

"You're not standing, you're pacing. And you are distracting me from my story." He suspected it would worsen her attitude. Nevertheless, he couldn't help but smirk when she glared at him.

"Drink that wine and sit down."

He thanked God the fire shooting from her eyes wasn't real, or his flesh would burn to a crisp. But she did what he told her, lifting her wine and throwing her head back to swallow it all. Then she leaned into the recliner.

"The flare almost worked. The thing released Ed, but it bounded out of the way of the shot, then came after me.

"I tried to reload, but the damned shells kept falling. I was trying to get one into the gun when claws dug into my back. I screamed as it turned me over. I knew I was about to die. The creature's nose almost touched mine as it sniffed me." Ryan finished off his glass of wine in a gulp and grimaced.

"Then I recognized him. My mind cleared and I knew who he was. Ugh didn't drown. He stood over me, dripping bloody saliva onto my neck.

"He laughed at me, taunted me in an awful, grating voice that bubbled up from his throat." Ryan looked directly into Lydia's eyes. "Then he lowered his head to my shoulder and ripped away a chunk of flesh."

"Oh, God." Lydia's hand covered her mouth, then slipped along her throat to her shoulder.

Ryan got up and knelt before her, taking her shaking hands in his. "I know."

She seemed to crawl into herself. He liked her better angry.

She lifted her face. "I was starting to think I imagined it."

"You didn't imagine it." He rubbed her arms.

"It's the same man."

"Yes."

"Ugh is the Butcher, but it's not a man. Oh." She lifted a hand to his face, her fingers igniting a trail of flame over his stubble. "You were attacked by him, too."

Her breath caressed his face even as her hand landed lightly on his chest. Heat radiated from her body. He'd knelt in front of her to comfort her, but now he wanted to ravage her. Nibble those luscious lips. Dig his fingers into her soft skin. He shook, fighting for control.

*

Lydia's heart went out to him. Kneeling before her, his head bowed, Ryan's body shook. She reached for him, wrapping her arms around him and pulling him tight to her chest.

He groaned, "Lydia." He ran his hands up her thighs then stopped.

Need overcame her. She tried to hold onto facts of the case, her anger at the Butcher, anything but the firm hands now skimming her back, and the hot breath panting against her neck. Thoughts slipped out of her mind like sand through her grasping fingers.

She clutched the tattered remnants of her control and whispered, "Ryan."

He raised his head and their eyes met. He struggled. She could see it. Biting her lip, she reached for his face and rubbed a hand up the coarse shadow on his cheek.

His nails gripped the small of her back. "I need to finish this," he said, his voice thick as he started to pull away.

"No!" She grabbed his shoulders and pulled him near. *Don't back away now.* Desperate, she crushed her lips on his, her tongue demanding entrance.

He met her assault with one of his own. She tasted wine on his lips. Even as she ripped his shirt from his shoulders, his possessive hand gripped the nape of her neck. She released a joyful moan when his other hand snaked up her skirt. His fingers tightened on her thigh, stopping short of her thong. Anticipation of his touch had her vision swimming.

Raking her nails across his back, she reared to look at him. Mouth swollen and eyes dilated, he licked at the blood she'd drawn when she bit his lip. They froze just a moment while their gazes met. Then he grinned, teeth and eyes gleaming.

Both of his hands slipped to her waist. Grasping, he slid her from the chair to the floor. She didn't land gently, but his power and control fired her further.

He loomed, the muscles in his chest rippling as he took hold of her top in both hands and ripped it in two. Exposed, her nipples hardened. He paused, looking at her breasts a moment before bending to nip at them. Lydia arched, groaning, aching for him to take more. To take her.

Instead, he shuddered and stood. Confused, mortified that he might mean to end it, she turned her head, closing her eyes. Part of her wanted to sink into the floor. Another part raged. She wanted him, and damn it, she would have him.

With a growl, she sat. Her fury softened slightly when he took off his belt. Impatient, she went to him and pushed aside his hands to unfasten his jeans. She ripped the boxers aside, snarling, and took his shaft in her hand. Like a rock wrapped in satin, the mass of it made her ache to have it inside her.

After seconds of letting her nibble and lick her prize, he pushed her to the floor and stretched out on top. Bruising and nicking her skin, his hold scratched and possessed. Teeth raked across her breasts, sending feverish chills through her.

They rolled, and she bit his shoulder, tasting salty sweat and the metallic flavor of blood.

"Now," she demanded. Her voice sounded coarse to her ears.

They rolled again and he entered her. She screamed as an explosion of pleasure washed through her. Meeting every thrust, her world tilted. Eyes closed, she wrapped her legs around him.

"Lydia." His gruff voice called through a fog. Arms encircled her, lifting her from the floor until she rode on his lap. Rough lips met hers, even as their hips pounded together. "Look at me," he ordered, pressing his forehead to hers.

She obeyed and focused on his eyes. The deep green of them enveloped her. Even as her body built to orgasm, they possessed her. Something in her mind connected, like a disjointed socket slipping into place. "We are one," she whispered.

"Yes," he panted.

Joined, she shared every delight he took from her. Every jolt of sensuous pleasure ran between them like an electrical current, swelling, until together, they detonated.

Chapter 16

Lydia lifted her head from Ryan's shoulder, taking all her strength. All energy, motivation, and rage of the past week drained and left her relaxed.

For the first time in her memory, she felt complete. A gaping breach she never knew existed became filled.

There hadn't been any steady men in her life, and she'd never thought she needed one. The brief interludes in her past were just that, intermittent periods of intimacy. Not real relationships.

Now, she sat on the lap of a man who held her, caressing her back with light fingertips and making every part of her tingle. She knew she would never be whole if they didn't stay together.

Rising, she kissed his ear. He stood and held her close for a moment before letting her go. She felt his stare as she left the room to get dressed.

When she reentered, heat rose inside her, reacting to his penetrating gaze. A cold streak ran down her spine. Uncomfortable, and alternating between flashes of heat and submersion in ice water, she racked her mind for something to say.

"Um." She poured another glass of wine and placed the empty bottle on the kitchen counter. Turning, she found his eyes still on her. Staring at her. Into her.

Having settled in the recliner, he'd raised the footrest and folded his hands across his lap. And watched her. What did he wait for? Becoming increasingly agitated, she shifted from one foot to the other. Finally, she couldn't take it anymore.

"What?"

No reaction at all.

"What?" she said louder. She trembled and noticed her voice

raised an octave. "Do you regret this?" She waved a hand at the floor they'd so recently vacated.

"Do you understand what just happened?" His eyes seemed to penetrate her soul.

"Shit, Ryan. I was here wasn't I?" She put her glass on the coffee table and flopped onto the couch. "I rather enjoyed it. What's the problem?" She couldn't look at him. Didn't he feel as good as she did? Didn't he enjoy it? How could he be so passionate one moment and so calculated the next?

Sure, a one–night stand, a quick romp in the sack to take the edge off, fine. But this was more. Oh, so much more. He had to see that. The glow warming her a minute ago dimmed, replaced with a cold chill.

Her mind started to fog. She fought against it. Tried to clear it. An image, like a daydream, started to form in her mind. The edges of the picture were grey and fuzzy, but in the center lay Ryan, spread eagle on ice. Dazed and confused, he rose. She felt his disorientation as easily as she felt the couch beneath her.

He called for his companions and searched for signs of the man who attacked him. He stumbled in the direction he thought a village might lay.

Time passed in the vision, and she sensed his hunger became nearly unbearable. He needed food. Off the ice now, he trudged through sparse trees and fields of snow.

At sunset, he discovered something lying in a bloody snow bank ahead—a human leg. He grabbed the dismembered limb and frantically took a bite. Frozen solid, the leg wouldn't give the smallest piece as he gnawed at it. Frustrated, he howled his rage and discarded it. Her blood raced in frustration for him.

He walked by the light of a full moon, following a smell he'd never noticed before. He pursued food. Tracking for hours, he hunted the source of the luscious aroma. Lydia started to salivate.

Then he came upon a campfire. Beside it sat an old man. Sled dogs tied to trees surrounding the camp growled as Ryan circled. The old man smelled so tasty. Ryan's mouth watered with anticipation. Bounding from the cover of the woods, he roared with hunger.

The old man jumped with fright and collapsed. Ryan sniffed his would-be dinner, revolted to find it dead already. Hungrily, he turned to the dogs. She ground her teeth, her body tensing as she lived the attack.

Ryan woke on the third morning, covered in blood and fur. The remains of the dogs surrounded him. In a flash, memory returned and he jumped to his feet in disgust. The old man's body lay nearby, now surrounded by the carcasses of his dogs.

Weeping at the monster he'd become, Ryan attempted to bury the dead man, piling snow over the body. Then he mournfully gathered the remains of the sled dogs and threw them in the fire.

"What the hell!" She jumped from the couch, heat rising to her face.

"I followed the old man's tracks in the snow back to a small town, and made it back to civilization soon after. That's the rest of the story." While she'd been entranced, he'd wandered to the window to peer out. Now he turned, his face impassive at her newfound rage.

"This is impossible," she sputtered, pacing again.

"Yes, well." He went to her and gripped her shoulders to hold her still.

"Werewolves don't exist!" She broke from his grip. "Ridiculous. Insane. No, there's some other explanation."

"Really? Do you have one for all the dead squirrels you slept with the other night? How you ended up at the zoo?"

"I chased the Butcher into the zoo."

"And simply decided to sleep there?" His amusement tickled at the edge of her mind, and she fought the urge to smile.

"How did you know about the squirrels?" She bowed her head, ashamed.

He closed the distance between them and sniffed her neck, sending electrical fingers of pleasure through her body. "I smelled them on you."

"Oh, God," she whispered as he kissed just under her ear. "This isn't real."

His hands gripped her hips and he pressed her to him. "You're going to have to get used to it."

She laid her palms against his hard chest. "Interesting words for a man who spent the last few years plotting revenge."

"Not revenge, exactly. And I've grown a lot in the past week or so." He kissed her tenderly. "This is our life, for better or worse."

"*Our* life? How can *we* have a life? They never have lives in the movies." She couldn't bring herself to say werewolf again. "They always lose their minds and kill themselves. They're racked with guilt."

"Guilt at killing innocent people." He took her head in his hands and looked in her eyes. "Have you killed anyone, Lydia?" When she paused, he added, "Since you were attacked?"

"No. Not if you don't count the squirrels and antelope." She shook her head. "It's hard not to count them."

"I know." He stroked her shoulders.

Holding on to him like a life raft and the only thing keeping her from falling into the depths of madness, she asked, "How come you didn't go crazy like Jacobs?"

"I did. Those first three days I was lost. But after the full moon ended and I hadn't managed to actually kill and feed on anyone, I was free. I was in the wilderness, away from civilization. There was no opportunity."

"After the full moon." She pressed her forehead against his chest and groaned, "Oh, God."

"Accept what you are, darling." He stroked her hair.

"Okay then, why haven't I gone crazy?" she asked, still nuzzled up to him.

His hand paused on her hair. "I don't know." He led her to the couch and reclined on it with her. "Perhaps because you're a woman. Perhaps because you had me here to ground you. Could be because you started the rabies shots."

The feel of his body stretched on the couch beneath her had a soothing effect on her nerves. "You think it could be a form of rabies?"

"You're the one that thought it could be a disease, Lydia. But I'm certainly not going to hand myself over to science so they can find out."

She snorted on a laugh. "Me, neither."

They lay in silence a moment, Lydia resting on his chest and listening to his heartbeat.

"Perhaps the drive is different for a female," he suggested. "It could be you're drive was to mate, not to kill."

"Unlikely. That doesn't explain the animals." She thought a moment. "That would be hunger, not murder." Another pause. "No, because if the drive was to mate, I would have thrown myself at you, and we would have done it the first night I stayed here."

"True," he acknowledged. "I've tried to study this on my own. Research werewolf lore." He squeezed her shoulder when she flinched at the word. "They focus on males. The urge to kill humans is overwhelming, at least through the first full moon. They say if you don't kill a human during your first full moon, you can beat the curse."

"You didn't."

"Yeah, well if I lived in the dark ages and I'd managed to get through without killing anyone, I wouldn't let them know some residual effects remain. Would you?" When she shook her head, he continued. "There are hundreds of theories on how to turn a werewolf human. I've tried most of them, and so far nothing's removed all the symptoms. Reflexes and sense of smell are heightened, and I still get irritable and lose my temper once a month."

Lydia couldn't help but laugh. "Welcome to the plight of every woman in the world."

He chuckled. "Yeah, well."

She thought back to his story. He had told her the second half without words. Jesus, she was slow. "Did you know you could send an image into my mind?"

"Projection. Ugh would torment me with visions when I got too close. He doesn't block his thoughts when he projects. Arrogant ass." He shrugged. "But it worked out well for us. I've never been able to, I guess *transmit* is the word, before. But I thought after we'd mated, we could communicate this way."

It made as much sense as the rest of it. And telepathy logically answered how pack animals communicated. Everything about this was surreal. Thinking about using supernatural abilities. Dealing with, hell, *becoming* a supernatural being. Mating with one. Wait a second.

"Mated?" She pushed up to look in his eyes, which twinkled with laughter. "That's not just sex, is it?"

His voice deep, his chest rumbled as he answered, "No, darling, it's not."

Never before had her heart soared and sank simultaneously. Too much, too fast. *Focus, damn it. Focus. One problem at a time.* But was it a problem? Didn't she want this? A companion? A partner?

No, not now. She needed to concentrate on the job. She only needed the job. Not this distraction.

Oh, but his embrace held such tenderness and welcome.

"All this new information is enlightening, but doesn't get me close to taking down the Butcher." She traced a finger around his chest, outlining every muscle through his T-shirt.

The warmth of his arms felt better than a warm bath. It took concentration to form a coherent thought and not sink into him. Even then she felt herself slipping.

"I can't think like this." She kissed the stubble on his chin and made to stand.

He wrapped his legs and arms tightly around her. "Don't think," he said, kissing and sniffing the top of her head. "Weren't you ordered to rest a few hours?" His fingers pressed into tense spots on her shoulders and back.

"Hmm," she agreed, starting to relax and shutting out one of the warring voices in her head. "Who am I to disobey orders?" She mumbled the words into his chest and drifted to sleep, lulled by Ryan's heartbeat and talented fingers.

*

He paced the concrete floor. Bitch should have been alone. He growled and swiped at the man who cowered before him. He wanted her alone. He wanted to snatch her and bring her here.

He lowered to the terrified man's face. Nothing the man said made sense. What good is groveling when you couldn't understand it? Even the scent of his fear smelled off. Corn chips. Just wrong. He resumed his course across the warehouse floor.

He paced, liking to think of himself as BB. He had no home. He settled anywhere that wasn't occupied. Warehouse, abandoned store, empty house. Didn't much matter as long as he had a place to brew his income. After all, a guy couldn't live off terror alone. He grinned and licked his lips.

As long as he could remember, he'd created concoctions for those who needed a little pick-me-up. Those people would be lost without someone like him. They couldn't be constructive members of society without his brew. And if they happened to abuse it, well, that wasn't his problem.

And since that beautiful night they picked up the drugged hitchhiker, BB'd never had to sample his own merchandise again.

He wanted to tell the tale. He wanted to tell that bitch cop. But instead, he needed to work with what he had, and hunkered down in front of the little foreign man.

"You want to know how I became invincible?" He poked a clawed finger at the cringing man. "Huh?"

More babble.

"Well, I'll tell you anyway." He grinned and the man shrieked.

"One night, years ago, me and my buddy were driving to . . ." he smacked the babbler on the top of his head. "Pay attention."

BB cleared his throat. "Anyway, we were in his car, just driving along, getting stoned. We see this bum on the side of the road. He's all hunched over and dirty and hairy and stuff.

"I don't know what we were thinking. He obviously didn't have any money to steal. Or buy our stuff with, or anything. And God knows we weren't interested in helping the bastard. But there was something about him that made it impossible for us to just drive by. So we pull over and are just like, 'Where to?' ya know?"

BB got into his story now. Although his captive struggled with the ropes that bound him, BB didn't pay him much mind, except to poke at one of the brown bare feet.

"This guy smelled rank. Like he spent days in the sewer. My buddy says, 'Damn man, you stink. Get the fuck out of my car.' And I'm like, 'Yeah, get out.' The smell was totally ruining my buzz.

"But this guy grips the back of my buddy's seat and tells him to drive. Well, he gets going, and I'm like nervous now. This dude had claws. He says he's looking for a special type of guy. I'm like 'No way pal. I like girls, dig?'" He poked at the foot again. "Get it?"

More incomprehensible babbling.

"Damn man, you should've learned English. Anyway, the dude laughed like a bumper scraping gravel and said he liked me. I'll admit I was freaked out. Then he dove over the seat and bit me. Just bit my shoulder, just like that," he said with a snap of his fingers. "And I black out.

"When I woke up, everything was bright. The full moon was out and I just lay there and stared at it. I stood up and I was powerful. Perfect. And I knew I would always be perfect. I look around and the guy is gone, but there is my buddy, trapped in his car. He's all stuck behind the wheel, and all I can think is, damn he looks tasty." BB licked the tan foot.

His captive shrieked.

"Just like you, corn chip. You look tasty. You can't understand me anyway. This isn't as fulfilling as I'd hoped." He considered the babbling face. "I was given a gift that night. I've passed it on to some because I knew it would destroy them, and to others because, like me, they were worthy. Now I'm home and it's time I mated."

He waggled his bushy eyebrows and grinned. "Already picked out the bitch." His smile fell. "Gotta get rid of the other one first, but sometimes entertainment can make me hungry." He gnashed his teeth as he said the last word and the little man fainted.

With a barking laugh, he set about rousing his dinner. This morsel didn't deserve the gift. Now wasn't the time to eat lightly, he'd eat all of this little corn chip.

*

In his dingy apartment, Detective Kevin Henson closed the bathroom door of his studio apartment to develop his film. He hadn't been invited on the operation at the clubs the evening before, so instead, he followed covertly.

Since childhood, Henson always enjoyed playing spy. Cloak-and-dagger games thrilled him to no end. He would carry a notepad and his 35-millimeter camera everywhere, attempting to find and solve mysteries.

He wore disguises and practiced speaking with foreign accents when his mother brought home her johns. Finally, he grew up and graduated. He'd studied hard, his ticket out of his filthy life.

He applied to the CIA, his dream. He wanted to be a spy. But after all the tests and interviews, they rejected him. He lacked stability enough to work for them. They said that. Not stable.

So he tried his hand at private detective work. He did as well as he knew he could. After a while, chasing cheating spouses didn't thrill him anymore, so he applied for the police force.

They let him in, and knowing it was as close to his dream as he could get, he worked hard. Everyone had to know how good he was. He wanted notoriety, fame. He wanted everyone in the area to know him as the best.

But that woman, Lydia Davis, got the good cases. So what if she got it because of seniority? Reporters had already interviewed her on the case more than once. Bitch. Those fifteen minutes belonged to him. She didn't deserve it. He hung up wet photos to dry.

Just look at her, rubbing all over that reporter. She wants fame; all she has to do is sleep with some horny reporter. Slut.

He worked himself up, but if he intended to oust that bitch from her favored position, he'd need to play it smart. Play it cool. Closing his eyes, he breathed deeply. He smoothed his hair, and studied the drying photographs.

Chapter 17

Waking several hours later alone on the couch with a blanket tucked around her, Lydia called for Ryan and received silence in response.

She stretched, pointing her toes and lifting her arms over her head. Relaxed as she hadn't been in months, she gazed around, possessive about her new home. After a moment, she realized that though she had no hand in the decorating, she wouldn't change a thing.

She liked the natural, warm, and inviting colors and furniture. The scent, a mixture of soap from their showers, leftovers from dinner, and the musk of their passionate lovemaking pieced into a comforting quilt, making her safe and warm.

Hungry, she raided the fridge. Eating cold Chinese leftovers at the counter, she jerked at the scrape of a key in the lock. By instinct, she reversed the fork and stepped toward the door. Then tendrils of Ryan's thoughts met hers. She couldn't extract details, but like her, he focused on food. Relaxing, she went back to her meal.

A pizza box topped with two Styrofoam containers preceded Ryan through the door. Grinning, he eyed her as he set the box on an empty section of counter. A canvas bag he'd slung over his shoulder sagged with books and papers, and he leaned it against the wall by the door.

"Thought you'd be hungry." He chuckled as he tossed empty takeout cartons in the garbage.

"Ravished," she replied, dumping the remaining contents of the last carton into her mouth in an unladylike manner. Didn't matter though. He understood, and she sensed his amusement.

"This could be cool." She grinned and handed him a soda.

"The mind reading or the uncontrollable eating?"

"Both, I guess. As long as I don't gain weight from the eating."

She moved the Styrofoam containers and lifted the pizza box lid, grabbing a slice loaded with everything. "And being a couple has to be easier when you have a mental link with your partner." She laughed. "I never thought I'd say something like that."

"You seem relaxed." He leaned a shoulder against the wall.

"Like I haven't been for ages."

"Euphoria?"

"I guess you could say that," she answered around a mouthful.

"Have you thought of work yet?"

"Why should I?" She tossed the crust in the garbage and reached for another. Before her fingertips cleared the edge of the box, Ryan caught her wrist. "Hey!" she yelled, trying to pull away.

"You, darling, are getting too comfortable." He kissed the palm of her hand. "A reaction to mating."

"What? How would you know?" She glared at him. "Like a woman gets married and lets herself go? It's only been six hours, for crying out loud." She tugged her hand free. "I thought you understood me. What I'm going through."

"I do. The problem is, *you* don't."

Dumbfounded, she gaped. How dare he! She stepped, teeth and fists clenched to contain instant inflaming rage at his impertinence. A flash of an idea occurred to her that she reacted irrationally, but she shoved it impatiently aside and glowered at Ryan.

"So much for avoiding misunderstandings," he muttered, rolling his eyes. Gripping both her wrists, he braced them behind her back.

Aroused by his show of dominance, the rage dissipated. She leaned into him, ignoring the pressure it put on her shoulders. She nuzzled and nipped his neck.

He continued to talk, but she only half listened while reaching for his earlobe with her tongue.

"Since I met you, I've looked into what could happen if we . . ." He groaned as she nibbled his ear. "This isn't you."

"Oh, I think it is." She ground her hips against him and raised a knee to rub the inside of his thigh. *So damned sexy*. Arching her back, she licked her lips and tried to project the image of her hard nipples and the warm wetness between her legs into his mind.

"Hormones," he panted, releasing her wrists. He struggled, closing his eyes and breathing deeply. "You can't think past your own immediate needs. We shouldn't."

She could see the fight within him and she licked her lips, rubbing her hands down his body to turn the tide of the war. "I want you," she growled into his ear. "Take me, hard and fast. Now."

They both heard the snap of his control. As she ripped at his pants, his hands had already found their way inside her clothing. One rubbed a nipple between thumb and forefinger; the other caressed the curve of her hip.

Impatient, she wanted him inside her. She stepped and wriggled out of her pants, wanting nothing in his way. Then gripping his shoulders, she lifted herself onto the counter, pushing the containers to the edge where they threatened to topple onto the floor.

He stepped forward, spreading her thighs wide. He started to crouch, lowering his head for a taste.

No! She clutched at his shirt. At his hair. Her head fell back, her eyes closed. Even the spectacular sensations tested her patience.

"No." She managed to gasp. "Now!" She wrapped her legs around his waist and pulled him to her. Finally, he entered her with untamed abandon.

"Yes!" She wanted this. Savage passion. Convulsive completion. "Yes!"

The pace still quickened. All thought gone. Nothing existed but the two of them and the friction, the ultimate sensations that coursed through her. Their rhythm keeping pace with their racing heartbeats. Until, with an explosive conclusion, they finished together.

She clung to him, holding on while the world righted itself. As she started to regain her senses, she kissed his chest and delighted in smelling the combination of his cologne, sweat, and sex.

"Wow," he said, wearing only a goofy grin.

Her appetite sated for a moment, she slid off the counter and delivered him a heady kiss before dressing. "Okay," she said, caressing his chest, feeling a smile spread across her face as wide as the Cheshire Cat's. "I'm listening now."

Moving aside so she could pass, he said, "Just a minute to remember what I was saying." He tugged his clothes into position.

Still smiling, she listened to him rattle around in the kitchen while she moved to the large living room window to peer through a crack in the drapes. She needed to focus on something, but like a freshly caught fish, the thought slipped from her grasp the harder she tried to hold on.

"You were talking about the research you've done," she prompted.

"Yes, well. You've heard that some animals mate for life?" He paused, so she nodded. "Once they do, their life functions change and they instinctively fall into another role."

She nodded again and said, "I saw something on the nature channel once that talked about how male lions travel in packs, but once they mate, the male protects the home and the female hunts, or something."

Outside, rush hour began. The coffee shop placed dinner specials on the board outside.

Behind her, the clank of plates made her turn. "Okay, so you're telling me I'm behaving this way because I'm a, *you know*, and my new instincts say I need to stay home and be a breeding machine who protects the den from invaders."

"Exactly."

"Insane. This whole thing is insane."

She turned as he set a tray on the coffee table. Arranged in two layers, the first held assorted sushi and bite–sized servings of steak tartare topped with onions and capers on small squares of lettuce.

The top tray held another assortment. This one of pastries filled with chocolates, jellies, and a variety of creams she could see from little holes in the sides. Her mouth watered and the barely quenched hunger flared at the scent.

She went to the couch and sank onto it. Then she slipped to the floor, kneeling reverently in front of the fragrant delicacies.

"Marry me," she whispered. Realizing Ryan surely heard, she glanced up and stammered, "Ah. Um. Ah . . . "

The corner of his mouth twitched. "Is that something you want to do? A ceremony?"

She shook her head. Where had that come from? *Good God, get a grip.*

She could accept their bond. They would be together forever. But a ceremony with flowers, music, and a caterer was something she couldn't handle. Not at the moment. She shook her head again.

"Then I'm content." He knelt beside her and lifted a sushi roll to her lips. "For now." At her hum of pleasure, he smiled. "I picked this up from a catering shop around the corner. Appetizers ready to order."

The rice and fish practically melted on her tongue. While the beast in her longed to gobble it, she fought the urge. She'd lost control too often already today.

"Okay, so what should I do about this instinct?" she asked around a taste of steak.

Peering at the top tray, he replied, "Tonight is the last night of the full moon. I think everything will calm down for you tomorrow." He popped a pink powdered pastry into his mouth. "Oh, these are good." He picked another and held it out to feed her. "My rage faded after my first full moon. It comes back, but it's controllable. I haven't lost control like that in a very long time."

She lifted a bright pink piece of sushi and considered his words. "It's not like a bad temper. It's more like being taken over by a monster."

"Yes," he agreed, caressing her thigh while selecting his own morsel.

"I can't risk leaving the apartment by myself. Until this is done, I'm a danger to everyone I come in contact with."

"You can take it out on me." He waggled his eyebrows.

The weight of her worry lifted briefly as she laughed and smacked his arm playfully. "Seriously, though, I have to think of something to tell the chief. I certainly can't tell him the truth." She tapped her long beautiful nails on the coffee table, struck once again by their perfection. She spread her fingers wide. "At least my nails are stronger now." She made a clawing motion.

"There are several benefits to our situation. At least I've noticed several." At her raised eyebrow he explained, "The ability to see in the dark, for example. Our kind appears to be mostly nocturnal."

She tried not to shudder at the words *our kind*.

"We also have a heightened sense of smell."

She lifted a sushi roll and sniffed. "Yum." Then she tucked her tongue into her cheek. "Can't be good on the subway."

The corner of his mouth quirked. "It's worse in a port-a-john."

Covering her mouth, she giggled around the sushi.

"Increased strength." He grinned at her raised eyebrow. "Not like we've turned into the Hulk or anything, but you should be careful. Instead of giving someone a black eye, you could crack their skull."

Nodding, she polished off the last of the steak. "Our appearance isn't what I expected. I thought there would be more hair and longer teeth."

He caressed her cheek. "You get it at night."

"What?" She pressed her hands to her face. "At the clubs last night? Oh, God, I had a beard?" Mortified, she rubbed her skin. Was she going to have to shave now? Everything felt normal.

Ryan gripped her hands. "It's lighter than your hair and made you look tanned. It feels like satin, and in the lights of the club, it glittered like body paint."

She wanted to enjoy the compliments, but the idea of fur repulsed her. "It will be over tomorrow," she whispered.

"Shame." His deep green eyes darkened as he leaned to kiss her cheek. "You looked very sexy last night." She didn't believe him. How could a furry woman be sexy? She shook her head.

His mind reached out for hers.

She saw herself in last night's outfit, moving to a rhythmic beat. Her body glowed as she danced in roving multicolored lights. She *did* look good. But better than that was the reaction she felt in him while *he* watched her. More than love. Possession, passion. An all-encompassing desire overwhelmed him as he approached her.

Breathless, she removed her mind from his and opened her eyes. She hadn't realized she'd closed them. "Oh," she moaned slightly, kissing him. "Thank you." She moved her lips softly against his.

He nipped her lip. "As for your teeth, they erupt when you get irritated." He moved his collar for her to see a swiftly fading bruise. "Or aroused."

She gasped at the mark she'd obviously given him in the kitchen only moments ago.

"We also seem to be fast healers."

"Thank God for that." She ran fingertips over his neck.

"I'm fine." He laid his hand over her trembling one. "You should call in and tell them you're sick."

"No." Her laugh sounded lighter than her actual mood. "It's not like I work retail. I can't just call in sick."

He nodded and handed her the phone.

She decided to call Adams.

Slightly panicked, she listened to the ringing. What could she say? Not the truth. *I'm too moody to come in because I'm turning into a werewolf, and if someone pisses me off I'm likely to rip off their head.* No, that wouldn't work.

Once she heard Adams' voice on the other end, her mind cleared and she knew exactly what to say. "Adams, it's Davis. Listen, I got some new information from our tipster."

"Great," he replied. She heard rustling papers. "Go."

"Okay. Check out reservations for an ice fishing excursion made at the Winter View Lodge and Spa three years ago January. The report probably says a guide and two of the guests were attacked and killed by an animal. I need all the background information you can find on the guests who were attacked. I mean *everything*. Get permission to open their minor records, if there are any."

"That's going to be tough, Davis. You can't just go peeking into sealed records."

"That's why you'll need permission. One of the guests was the Butcher. I know it."

He sighed. "All right. I'll look into it. Are you okay?" he asked, concern deepening his voice.

"Couldn't be better." She smiled at Ryan who moved to take the trays into the kitchen. "I'm great. Give me a call if you get anything. I'm going to do some digging of my own from here."

"A reporter, Davis. Really?"

She delighted in hanging up on him.

From the kitchen, Ryan asked, "So what do you want to do now?"

She stood and sauntered to the counter. "Later, I need to get online to see what I can learn."

"And now?"

"Now I have other ideas." She grabbed his shirt, getting a sexy, throaty laugh from him as a reward, and pulled his lips to hers.

*

Henson tapped on the chief's door. He waited, shifting folders from one hand to the other. He needed to report on a domestic homicide, but he also needed to discuss the pictures he held in his hands. It was time to make his case against Davis. Perhaps if he knew what kind of woman worked for him, the chief might remove her from such a sensitive case.

When he heard the chief's bellow, he opened the door and stepped inside. *Tread carefully. Be sensitive.* After all, she probably slept with him, too, and who would want to get rid of his piece at work? That's why the pictures were so important. Henson covered his smile with a cough.

"Henson," the chief greeted.

Nice enough, dullard. Too bad such a worthless cripple ran the department. If a real man ran the precinct, the whore would have gotten fired long ago.

"Chief, got that report for you on the domestic homicide. Wife poisoned the husband because he was cheating with the babysitter."

Fairweather took the file and glanced over the report. "Good work." He waited a beat, and when Henson remained still, asked, "Is there something else?"

"As a matter of fact, sir, there is." He passed Fairweather the other file. "Sir, regarding Detective Davis. It is my opinion she is not fit for duty. She doesn't conduct herself with the dignity required for a detective on such a high-profile case."

Fairweather flipped through the photographs. With each one, his face turned a deeper shade of red. *That's it. Enraged that his piece is getting it somewhere else.* Henson fought the sneer that threatened to take over his face.

"What is this?" the chief demanded, glaring. "Did you follow on the op last night?"

Henson's mouth dropped open. This wasn't how it was supposed to go.

"You followed her, took pictures of her undercover, and are now trying to push them on me like she's unfit? She's undercover," he said slowly, pronouncing every syllable. "That's something you're familiar with. Right, detective?"

"Ah yes, b-b-but . . ." Henson stammered. Didn't he see what a slut she was? "Sir, if she hadn't been cavorting with that reporter, she would have caught the Butcher."

"That so? Apparently *you* were there. Where were you? As it was, she was the only one of you officers that kept up with him."

"She lost him," Henson argued.

"We found traces in the sewer. *She* got us a lead." Fairweather leaned back in his chair, fury draining from his face. "Henson, you are not on the Butcher case. You are to keep away from Davis, and from any of her evidence."

Henson stepped toward the door.

"I know you are attempting to undermine Detective Davis. That behavior is not acceptable in my department. If you continue to intercept her reports, you will be suspended. Am I clear?" The deep voice cracked like a whip.

"Yes, sir," Henson said and backed out of the office entirely. Once he'd moved a safe distance from the door, he muttered, "Tattling bitch."

Chapter 18

Adams worried for Lydia when they disconnected. Not for Detective Davis. She could handle herself. No, he worried for Lydia, the woman. The one who had few friends. The one who took almost everything to heart, even if she didn't show it. In the years they'd worked together, he'd never known her to be serious about anyone. Sure she dated, but just brief liaisons. More often than not, the guys she left reeling from a breakup came to him for advice. Invariably, he told them to move on.

This time, she seemed head–over–heels for a hotshit reporter. Adams wanted happiness for his friend, but with all the stress, he wondered if she could really think clearly. Especially with some guy coming in and sweeping her off her feet.

Although he found Detective Davis attractive, Adams never thought of her that way. Sure, he had made a pass at her to keep up appearances. However, if she'd said yes, he would have found an excuse, and quickly. He just couldn't date a woman who seemed more like a sister.

His mother met Davis once at a precinct picnic. She took to Davis instantly. Since then, his mother constantly hinted they were both single, attractive adults. He spent hours explaining the idea was impossible.

He settled into his home office to start the search. He could go to the precinct, but the tech guys had come over and installed all the latest security and data search tools. So instead of driving, he crossed the room to his desk in ratty sweat pants and a Grateful Dead T-shirt.

He checked his notes, then pulled up info on the Winter View Lodge in Vermont. The first picture on the lodge's website was a money shot of the log exterior in winter against the mountain view at twilight. Windows glowed orange, welcoming and warm. He snorted. *Should be on a postcard. Probably is.*

The cat, still without a name, jumped onto the desk and bumped his head against Adams' hand. Not to be distracted, he scratched behind the cat's ears with one hand, exploring the site with the other.

Luxury rooms . . . spa services . . . Aha! Outdoor activities. Another list showed cross-country skiing, carriage rides, ice skating, ice fishing. He checked his notes again and selected ice fishing. The screen changed, listing guided day trips onto Mixon Lake. Writing the phone number for excursion registration, he decided to leave the site and look for news reports on any tragedies at the lodge or on the lake.

More than a hundred articles appeared—everything from hypothermia to drowning. "This needs to be pared down a bit," he muttered to the cat as his fingers tapped the keyboard. On the desk, the cat pricked an ear, and then turned to lick himself.

"Yeah, I see how interested you are," he said to the back of the cat's head.

The screen changed and new search results appeared. The very first article, "Ice Fishing Tragedy, Only One Survivor," appeared promising.

"On Mixon Lake early this morning, rescue crews arrived to a grisly sight. In what appears to be an animal attack, two tourists and their guide were brutally mutilated. Names are being withheld until next of kin have been notified.

"One survivor has been found nearly five miles from the scene of the attack. In shock and dehydrated, the man managed to lead a rescue and retrieval team to the general area where he and his group had been fishing.

"The survivor, Ryan Williams, a sports reporter, routinely participates in and reports on extreme sports. He is receiving medical treatment and is said to be in good condition."

Adams's mouth dropped open. *Well, well. Our mild-mannered reporter is a survivor of a tragedy that took the lives of three people.* Did Davis know about this? He fought the urge to call her and insist she spend the night at a hotel.

He needed more information. Could be Williams actually *was* a victim. "I need to see the police report," he said to the sleeping cat as he picked up the phone.

A brief call and a little charm had the primary investigator faxing the info to him. The case had been closed, but the investigator hadn't sounded totally convinced an animal had perpetrated the murders. After scanning the report, he called Davis.

When she answered, she sounded breathless and energized. Covering the receiver, he turned to the cat. "Wonder what she's been doing."

"Hey," he said. "Sorry to interrupt, but I just got the police report for the attack of the ice fishing crew."

"Great. Go," she ordered, all business now.

"Okay, according to the report, the only evidence they found led to a large animal. Black bear or mountain lion they assume, although the report notes that the carnage was excessive for an animal." She grunted in his ear, but he continued. "A search for the animal lasted several weeks and turned up nothing."

"I believe that." She snorted. "Okay, continue."

"The report lists the victims' names and a general summary for each.

"Martin Baker, fifty–nine, guide for Winter View Lodge and Spa for twenty years. Last residence listed as the Winter View Lodge. Highest level education, high school diploma. Survived by a brother and sister, both currently living in Montana. Victim confirmed using dental records.

"Edward Turner, forty-seven, credit services officer for Erintown Bank and Trust for ten years. Last resided with wife in their home in Erintown, Pennsylvania. His highest level of education was a Masters in Financial Management. Victim confirmed visually by wife.

"That would have had to suck," he added.

"Next." She sounded impatient.

"You know Ryan was there."

"Yes, damn it. I know that!" He heard deep muttering on her end. "Right." She took a deep breath. Adams could tell she wasn't talking to him. "You're right." She sighed. "Adams, I need to know the fourth." Her tone sounded measured, her words clipped. "Who was the other guy there?"

Normally with her this frazzled, he would find it almost impossible not to razz her. This time, he couldn't do it. "Robert Cooper, forty-two, no employment on record. Victim does have an extensive criminal record for drug possession and distribution. No record of finishing high school or GED. Get this: last known to live with his mother, Margaret, at 2352 Finch Street. Same neighborhood as the fire and Ms. Lenz."

"Good work. I want to interview the mother. We'll meet for breakfast and head over there together in the morning." Her voice moved away from the phone. Adams knew she spoke to Williams.

"Will do."

After hanging up, he lifted the summary for Ryan Williams. Only a couple things he didn't already know. College degree in journalism. Mother and father resided on a farm in upstate New York with their youngest son and daughter. Nothing about the reporter read false, yet Adams knew something wasn't right.

*

Lydia set the phone down and flashed Ryan a grin before reaching for his robe. Flinging the terry cloth over her bare shoulders, she strode from the bedroom for a victory snack.

"There's some leftovers in containers; I didn't put it all out," Ryan said. Music to her ears.

Quiet steps sounded behind her while she dug for the tub of leftover tartare.

"We have a lead and a name." She wriggled a little as she dipped two fingers into the meat and licked them clean.

"A name?" He reached a finger into the container only to yank it back when she growled.

He lifted an eyebrow. "Watch who you growl at."

She chuckled and offered him some off her own finger. "Robert Cooper, a local with a rap sheet for drug possession and distribution." She sucked another gob from her fingertip. "There was a meth lab in that abandoned house. I should have looked closer at the drug angle. We might have had him by now."

"You followed the relevant evidence."

"I don't need your platitudes," she snapped, tossing the empty container in the sink. "Twice I should have caught this bastard. I was within arm's reach. If I'd done my job better—"

"You thought you did get him, remember?"

"Yes." That was true, of course, but—

"You had no idea he escaped the burning house."

She closed her eyes. Rage bubbled, and she longed to take it out on him. "I know you're trying to help. And I'm trying not to be irritated with you, so let's just drop this."

He moved aside, but fixed her with a look that made her blood boil. Not trusting herself not to snap, she stood in the corner until she quieted her pounding heart. Breathing slowly, she focused on her toes until finally she felt calm enough to speak.

"Tomorrow, I'm going to meet Adams for a quick breakfast, and head over to Margaret Cooper's house. The mother. Question her, see if she has an idea where or what her son is. You're welcome to come."

In fact, she wanted him there, but she couldn't order him along. For the last few days, he'd followed her like a shadow. A glance to her side, and there he had waited. Protecting her, and all those around, from the beast inside her.

Technically, he had no business going. Reporters didn't ride along on an investigation. Hell, spouses didn't ride along. She could lose her badge by including him this way. Last night, she could explain away his presence as a cover. But his involvement should have ended there.

Still, she wanted him along. Leaving him behind was like leaving behind a limb. He had become part of her. She needed him. Needed him like she'd never needed anyone or anything before.

Suddenly her throat started to close and a weight settled over her. Tears filled her eyes as she gripped her chest to try to ease the throbbing. Drowning. Lost. Colored fog waved before her eyes. The room spun and she whimpered as she dropped to her knees.

Like a light in the darkness, Ryan came and eased aside the pain and pressure. "Shh." He cradled her against his chest. "You're not alone. I'll go with you."

"Can't," she managed to gulp out.

"Even if you didn't need me, I couldn't let you do this alone."

"I could get fired." The room started to swim. "I'm good at what I do. I help people." Too simplistic a comment. She'd helped hundreds of people by doing her job, and had the opportunity to do so much more good. She couldn't risk that. It wasn't just about her.

"Then we'll think of some other way to bring justice."

She peered into his eyes, and had no doubt they would find a way. Rising, she nodded. "Okay." The weight lifted and the fog cleared. Instantly she experienced a comforting surge of energy. "Okay," she said. "Let's talk about how we can take this bastard down." She paced to the window and back. "Is the whole silver-bullet thing real?"

Ryan pulled books from his sack by the door. "I picked these up on the way home, in case you wanted to do some research." He opened one and started flipping. "The general consensus is that silver will kill a werewolf. There are several ways that it is theorized a werewolf can be turned back human. In my experience, none of these work."

"Like what?"

"Like saying the werewolf's true name three times. I tried an experiment with my mother." He grinned. "I put a box of live toads on her counter then ran. She called after me, using every name—Ryan Michael Williams. She called three times before she screamed and ran after me."

"Ran after you?" Lydia glanced up from the index of a particularly large book.

"Yeah, one of the toads hopped out of the box and into her dish water. It took half an hour to round up all the toads and get them back outside."

Lydia smiled, shaking her head, and returned her attention to the index. She noticed an entry. Killing. She turned to the page and read aloud.

"Silver is the most common way to kill a werewolf. However, several sources, blah–blah, say it is possible that the term silver was mistranslated and could mean quicksilver, or mercury. Beware, mercury is very toxic to humans."

She scanned the next page and read again. "Werewolves have tremendous healing capabilities. So once you have disabled it with your silver/quicksilver bullet or spear, you then need to crush the brain and impale the heart with a wooden stake." Bewildered, she paused.

Ryan looked up. "Some people say that once you kill a werewolf, if you don't destroy the head and heart, the being will rise again as a vampire."

"There are such things as vampires?"

His face became pained. "Are you really asking me that?"

"Have you met one?" She couldn't help getting excited.

"Yes. There's an underground club for all us supernatural beings. I really should take you there." He ducked as she tossed a couch cushion.

"Smartass."

"If we exist, who knows?" He shrugged. "I don't think it's true, though. Jacobs didn't turn into one . . . that we know of."

Her eyes widened as she grabbed the phone and called the coroner's office. "Dr. Hoodam's office," she requested when the receptionist answered.

"Doctor. It's Detective Davis. I'm following a lead. Can you tell me if Hank Jacobs has been released for burial yet?"

"In the morning, he is to be transferred to the funeral home." An odd clanging sounded in the background.

"Could you tell me if his skin is sensitive to light?" The question sounded stupid, but she couldn't think of another way to get him to check the body.

Ryan leaned forward and mouthed, *what are you doing?*

"Detective, photosensitivity would cease at death," came his exasperated response.

"Could you please just check what happens to the skin under ultraviolet light?"

"What are you looking for?"

Good. She had piqued his curiosity. "Any reaction. I'll wait." She tapped a nail on the receiver, and glanced at Ryan who just shook his head. "Just want to see if he's still where he's supposed to be."

After a few moments, Hoodam returned to the phone. "There is no reaction, detective. Does that help you?"

"Yes, it does. Thanks." Hanging up before he could ask questions, she grabbed her pen and notepad and plopped onto the couch. "Okay, he's not a vampire. So the beating in the head and stabbing the heart is superfluous. We just need something silver . . . "

Damn. Even at her time of the month, she had never been this slow. "How did Jacobs die?"

He shielded something from her. He raised walls around his mind. She could see guilt on his face as he stared at her.

"The picture frame. What a coincidence the frame was silver."

"Yes."

"You killed him, Ryan." She gathered all the rage and frustration building inside and pushed them at him. He fell out of the chair as if she'd used her hands.

"I had no choice," he said, his voice gruff and deep as he stood, glaring.

She hunched, her hands out to her sides, and circled him. "You didn't try." She swiped at him, her nails catching his shirt, shredding like razors.

"This anger is the full moon affecting you, Lydia. Fight it. I did try with Jacobs. Let me show you."

Tendrils of his thought reach for her, but she slapped them away. "Don't touch me. You made yourself out to be this great man, able to withstand evil. But you're just a killer." Aware her words hurt him, she wanted to soothe him. Ease the sting. And yet, she wanted to rip him to shreds.

Howling, she lunged, this time raking his chest. Anticipating the move, Ryan gripped her throat and lifted her from the floor.

As she struggled, her robe opened. Taking advantage of his distraction, she kicked his throat and landed on top of him. He gasped for air, mouth opening and closing like a landed fish, but his eyes flashed with fury.

Abruptly, he wrapped her mind in rapport. Unlike the gentle links in the past, this connection was brutal. She screamed in his grip, forced to watch as Ryan tried to forge the link with Jacobs and how he killed him.

When he released her, she slid to the floor, spent and ashamed. Wrecked that she could accuse him of cold–blooded murder. *It's the moon. This isn't me.* She wanted to crawl and beg him to forgive her. That made her weak and she hated it.

The changes that should make her stronger sapped her strength. In place of the self–possessed woman lay a quivering heap of emotional discharge. No power. Only terrifying dependency and uncontrollable passions. *I've become pathetic.*

Prone on the floor, she examined the underside of the coffee table. She had attacked him. She couldn't make this right. The last shred of dignity gone, she wept. For herself. For Ryan. For a world innocent of the dangers around it. She wept.

After what seemed like hours, she calmed, though she still whimpered softly. A whistle pierced the silence. She jumped.

By her head, Ryan sat and observed her. "Are you finished?"

Like a slap across the face, the question cleared her mind. Taking a deep breath, she stilled. Drained and weak she faced him and nodded.

Gripping her chin, he pulled her lips to his. "I've never looked forward to a sunrise more."

Chapter 19

When Lydia awoke, she stretched languidly, her hand brushing across Ryan's chest. A sleepy chuckle rumbled in her ear as his arms hugged her, pulling her close. Muscles that carried her tension since the camping trip had relaxed.

"How are you feeling?" he breathed into her hair.

"Free." She snuggled closer, her legs caressing his. She stroked her palm over his chest as he leaned his lips to her ear.

"Good," he whispered, lowering his mouth to nibble an earlobe. Pleasure coursed through her like sunlight invading shadow. She moaned slightly in response.

Every touch left a trail of energy on her. He felt like warm satin under her lips. Her tongue drew a path up his neck, tasted the salt on his skin.

Holding her close, he gently rolled her onto her back. Then he slipped his hands along her sides and raised her arms over her head. She gripped the headboard and shut her eyes.

With them closed, the sensation of his fingertips tracing her arms to her sides made her gasp. Lightly he kissed her lips, throat, between her breasts. He eased lower and kissed her stomach. His hands glided down her hips, which she arched in welcome.

"Not yet." He pushed her flat and caressed the inside of her thigh with his mouth, slowly working his way down her leg. She moaned. It was delightfully excruciating.

He massaged each foot, gently squeezing the arches and pressing his thumbs in small circles. Ecstasy. He kissed each foot as he left it, and worked his way back to her mouth.

She breathed his name, her mind reeling.

"Darling." His voice sounded clear, yet heated with passion. "I want to make love to you."

She opened her eyes and smiled, wrapping her arms around him. "I want you, too."

When their lips met this time, she lost herself in him, in gentle caresses and loving nips. And when he finally entered her, he moved leisurely. Like to the rhythm of a slow song, they moved together, in a sensual dance. They crested as one in the dawn of their new lives together.

*

They met Adams at the diner for breakfast. The men ordered egg plates and dug in with relish. Lydia savored her coffee and a bowl of fruit, her voracious appetite having finally subsided.

They reviewed the information Adams collected about Margaret Cooper. A custodian at the elementary school for twenty-six years, she never married and had only one son.

Throughout the conversation, she noticed the looks Adams shot Ryan. She didn't need special powers to read his mind. He didn't trust the reporter. She considered confronting him, getting it out in the open, but thought it best kept for a private moment.

For all that the other patrons minded their own business, their attention would certainly shift her way if a heated discussion began. So when Adams cleared his throat, she hid a grimace behind her coffee mug.

"Look," he began," I don't know what's going on between the two of you, and I really don't want to know." He pointed at Ryan. "But as far as I'm concerned, you're a suspect. You don't belong in this interview." He managed to keep his voice in a conversational tone.

Impressive. Matching her tone to his and forcing a small smile, she said, "He's a victim."

"All the more reason for him to stay out of it."

180

She nodded. "Normally, I'd agree with you. This is different because he understands the nature of our killer. He spent time with him. More than anyone else, he can give us insight. We need to have him along."

Ryan raised an eyebrow at the officer. "I signed a waiver."

She glanced at Ryan. "Sorry about discussing you when you're sitting right there."

Adams ignored them. "What sort of insight?"

"I'll explain it later if it's necessary." She hated avoiding the subject, and she trusted him, but she had just come to terms with the change herself. She didn't need a scene.

"Fine," Adams said, lifting his mug and waving for the waitress.

*

Silence dominated in the car, putting Ryan on edge. Tension weighed heavily. Lydia drove, pursing her lips slightly in a way that, despite his position in the back seat, let him know she needed to share her secret with Adams. Ryan understood the sergeant was all but her partner. It seemed natural for her to tell him, and Ryan would support her.

But he suspected she probably wouldn't confide in him until they caught the Butcher. She'd do nothing to jeopardize the goal. Not nearly as obsessed as he with taking out the Butcher, she still wanted to catch him. It was enough.

Adams sat in the passenger seat, palming his knees, back rigid, and eyes twitching as he stared out the window. The sergeant concerned Ryan. Adams clearly didn't want him to have anything to do with Lydia, and used concern for the case as an excuse. Ryan couldn't tell the extent of the feelings this man had for her, and it didn't matter. He knew Lydia's heart, and while it held a place for Adams, the spot was designated for a friend. Just the same, he'd rather not have his back exposed to the officer, so he'd chosen the back seat.

Ryan didn't want to question Robert Cooper's mother. He just wanted to be there for Lydia, supporting her in case their quarry thought to visit.

He would also be able to tell if Ugh, as he still thought of him, already came home. Perhaps Lydia could, too, but he didn't want to take a chance she would ignore her new instincts. She was still a cop.

They pulled behind an old Volvo in the driveway of a one-story white bungalow. The immaculate yard, green grass smelling freshly cut as they walked across it, led to a woman in blue overalls who stooped, buried to the elbows planting a shrub.

As they approached, she glanced at Lydia and wiped bangs from her forehead, her gardening gloves leaving brown streaks in their place.

"Hello," she said, still crouched. "Is there something I can do for you?"

"Margaret Cooper?" Adams asked.

"Yes." A frown furrowed her filthy brow as she stood. Permed brown and grey hair framed her bright, yet guarded, green eyes. "And you are?"

"I'm Detective Lydia Davis." Leaving the introductions there Lydia extended her badge for inspection.

Ms. Cooper removed her gloves and extended a hand, which Lydia took as she used her other to tuck her wallet away. "What can I help you with, detective?"

"I need to ask you a few questions about your son, Robert."

The puzzled frown on Ms. Cooper's face appeared genuine as she welcomed them into her house and offered lemonade. The obvious wince on Adams' face when he declined made the corner of Ryan's mouth twitch.

She waved them to sit at a little table in the kitchen as she washed her hands and set out the refreshment. While their hostess bustled, Lydia caught Ryan's eye and raised a brow. He shook his head. The Butcher wasn't there.

When she joined them, Margaret Cooper directed them all with a piercing look. "What about my Robert?"

"Let's start with when you last saw him."

"Well, that's rude." The woman leaned against her chair back. "It would have been twenty-five years ago at his funeral, just before I put him into the ground."

"I'm sorry." Lydia shot a glance at Adams. "My information said he was still living."

"Lots of records got messed up when city hall went electronic. The paper has issues with it sometimes." Ryan sighed. *So close.* He stood; leaving his lemonade on the table then strolling around the kitchen, keeping his hands behind his back lest he give into temptation and punch something. He needed to move.

"Why did you want to know about my son?" Ms. Cooper asked as Ryan studied the picture gallery hanging on the kitchen wall.

"His name was on a hotel reservation three years ago. It's probable he was a victim of identity theft. We will look into it and take care of it for you. I'm sorry for bothering you."

Ryan listened with a heavy heart. Another dead-end. Always slipping past him. He ran a hand through his hair. Then something caught his eye. A young man, who appeared in most of the photos, standing next to a man with a protruding nose.

"Who's this?" Ryan pointed at the snapshot.

Ms. Cooper came to stand beside him. "Oh, that's Robbie and his friend Virgil. Virgil Miller. They were inseparable when they were in high school, until the accident . . . "

"What accident, Ms. Cooper?" Adams asked, his voice quiet.

"The one that killed my boy." She walked to the table and sat. "They were out with friends. I think they may have been drinking." Her voice hardened. "The police said they were on drugs, but I know better. My Robbie would never have done drugs."

"Was it a car accident, Ms. Cooper?" Lydia sat next to her and held her shaking hand.

She tried to be strong and compartmentalize her feelings into manageable bits, but that didn't make her less human, less compassionate. If it changed her like it changed him, becoming a werewolf could give her a new perspective on humanity.

"Yes, they said Virgil was driving. Their car crashed through the guardrail and rolled down the hill. The moon was full that night, so they should have been able to see the road. The police said there were no skid marks. That's why they said the boys were on drugs. They found my baby thrown from the car." Her face went red. "Shredded. The only part of him not torn to bits by the crash was his face."

"What did Virgil say happened?"

"Oh." Ms. Cooper dabbed at her eyes with a napkin. "Nothing. No one could find him. He lived with his grandparents. They had no idea where he ran off to."

"Thank you for your help, Ms. Cooper." Lydia shook her hand and motioned for the others to leave.

Ryan easily obliged. He didn't want to stay still for another minute. Virgil Miller. No way was this discovery another dead-end. The boy in that photograph was Ugh. He climbed in the back seat, drumming his fingers while Lydia slid behind the wheel.

Miller is the Butcher, used Cooper's name at the lodge, and who knows where else. Probably stole other identities too. "It's him," Ryan said once they got moving.

"Virgil Miller." Adams typed on the laptop plugged into the car's dash. "His grandparents are most likely dead." Everyone held a breath while the page loaded. "Wow, the kid got arrested five times between age eighteen and the accident two years later." He turned toward Lydia and smirked. "Guess what for?"

"Drug possession with intent to distribute," Lydia guessed.

"We have a winner. Sold marijuana first, then just before the accident, lysergic acid diethylamide. Rap sheet practically echoes Robert Cooper's."

"What's *lysoger*–whatever?" Ryan asked.

"LSD," Lydia explained. "Acid."

"And she thought her son was a good boy. How did she *not know* he didn't graduate?" asked Adams.

"Some parents don't like to admit their kids are in trouble. Means they did a shitty job," Ryan said. "Even if it means they overlook the obvious."

Lydia's eyes met his in the rearview mirror. "She didn't seem to know much about Miller. I'd like to see a report of the accident." She tapped her nails on the steering wheel. "Ryan, does the paper keep photos from a story they don't actually run?"

"Yes. Sometimes the story will expand and they're needed. Occasionally, we get something that the police requests later." He grinned.

"I'll drop you off at the paper while we go by the office."

Fantastic. He needed to be in motion. Digging through files in the archive might not be finishing off Ugh, but it moved him one more step in that direction.

When they pulled in front of the *Daily Times* building, Ryan leaned between the seats to kiss Lydia lightly on the lips. Then he turned to Adams. "None for you," he said, inches from the cop's face. The sergeant made a faint strangling sound as Ryan got out.

Chapter 20

When they pulled away from the curb, Adams cleared his throat. Lydia knew he wanted to talk about her relationship with Ryan. He had something personal on his mind. Otherwise, he would have just come out and said it.

Bracing for an outburst, she said, "Okay, get it out of your system."

"What do you really know about this guy?"

She laughed. "Quite a bit, actually." Leaning toward him, she whispered, "I know his deepest, darkest secret, Eric." Then she straightened. "Don't worry."

Crossing his arms, he muttered, "Just the fact he has a deep, dark secret worries me." His gaze bore into her, and he arched an eyebrow. "Seriously. Getting it on with a victim of an active case isn't like you. Don't you think it's too personal?"

"No." She kept her voice mild. "You're the one who's keeping Ms. Lenz's cat. One could argue that's personal. The cat should have been sent to the animal shelter."

When he didn't say anything, she patted his knee. "Neither one of us is compromising the investigation. As long as we keep our objectivity, I don't see a problem." She stopped at a light and added, "Look, let's just go talk to Sare in vice. He owes me a favor, and I think he'll be able to recognize Miller."

"Okay." He nodded slowly.

At the precinct, they took the stairs to the vice squad on the second floor. They needed to speak to someone who could remember busting Cooper and Miller, meaning they needed to talk to Anthony Sare.

The aging man ran a hand through salt–and–pepper hair when he saw them approach. "Look Adams, I don't have time for a poker game. They promoted me." He squinted and pushed thick glasses lower on his nose, then waved at papers stacked over his desk.

"Tough break." Lydia nudged a hip onto a sliver of desk.

Sare was the poster boy for getting the job done. When his wife passed away a few years ago, he threw himself into his work. More drug dealers met with convictions in the three years following her death than in the six years before. Even before his spree, Sare had a reputation for good police work. He would joke that he had so many commendations, he could paper the bathroom with them.

She thought it a shame when they pulled him from street duty. The fiery passion his eyes used to hold had dimmed to embers. "How'd it happen?"

"Damn physical. Said my eyes weren't good enough anymore. Unsafe for me to be on the street." He waved his hands over the desk in a grand sweeping gesture. "So they make me captain and sit me here until I go blind from pushing papers all day."

Adams patted his own belly. "Looks like it agrees with you, Sare."

The old man snorted and rubbed the bulge poking over his belt. "Burnt coffee and stale doughnuts."

They all laughed. "Yeah, that'll do it." Lydia rested a hand on one of the piles and leaned in. "Look, Sare, we need your help."

"This about the Butcher case?" He raised his eyebrows.

"I think so. Do you recognize the name Virgil Miller?"

"Miller, Miller." He rolled his chair and dug through one of the file cabinets behind his desk.

"Or Robert Cooper?" Adams added.

"Ah." He stopped digging and raised a finger. "Cooper and Miller. Dynamic Duo. Cooper was killed in a wreck a few years back."

Sare knew them. Elation filled her, and if it hadn't been completely inappropriate, she would have turned to Adams and said, "Told you so."

He rolled to the desk. "What do you need to know?"

She kept her face schooled in a somber expression. "Have you had any activity from Miller lately?"

"Trafficking?" asked Sare.

Lydia nodded. "Crystal meth."

"Haven't heard the name. We did have a handful of users in the hospital in the past few days. Every damn one of them claiming to have the flu, if you can believe that." He shook his head. "No one would rat out their old supplier."

Adams pursed his lips. "If their supplier got taken out in a fire, let's say." He caught Lydia's eye. "A few days would have given the junkies time to use up their stash and start withdrawal."

"Most junkies have a backup supplier," she said.

Adams shrugged. "That's why only a handful ended up in the hospital."

Sare bounced slightly in his chair. "You think it's Miller?"

"That's the theory." She tapped a fingernail on the pile of papers. "If I gave you a recent description of Miller, could you get it out to the people the department has undercover. We need to find his new base of operations."

"To set up another sting?" Adams smirked and crossed his arms. "We've done well with that so far."

Such a smartass remark needed a reaction, so she used one she learned from his mother. She stared at him, meeting his gaze easily until he finally averted his eyes. It took all the control she could muster not to smile when, out of the corner of her eye, she saw Sare shudder.

"Another raid. With a much smaller force." She lifted a hand as both men started to speak at once. "The larger raid started a fire last time and provided him with the distraction he needed to escape. There will be no distractions this time. No bait. This time he goes down." She smacked her palm on the desk.

Adams asked, "You'll pass the description around then?"

The older man ran another hand through his already disheveled hair. His eyes recovered some of their old passion. "Yeah. Yeah, I will."

She nodded. Sare would spread the word. One of the good things about being in the force for years, he knew everyone and accumulated many favors. He'd call them in, if only to catch the one that got away.

She turned to Adams to say as much when the booming voice of the chief called to her. The short, thin man limped toward her, his face hard as stone.

He dismissed Adams with a look, and returned his firm gaze to her. Unsure of the cause of his wrath, she started to give him an update on the case.

He held up a hand and motioned her to follow. And although the leg marred his gate, he set a quick pace. They didn't head for the elevator and his office as she'd assumed. Instead, they turned a corner into internal affairs.

"What is this, chief?" she asked, silently thanking God she'd finished her transformation.

"This." He turned and moved so close to her face she could feel his breath as he talked. "This is what happens when you ignore office politics. You haven't been in the office lately."

"Sir, I've been continuing the investigation. I've kept you appraised in my reports." She met his eye and didn't retreat.

"Unfortunately, there is more to the job than just doing your job." He moved toward the internal affairs conference room. Glancing over his shoulder, he said, "You've done your job well and no one is faulting you for that."

She held her ground, refusing to follow. "Sir, if I am to receive a formal interview, I was to be notified in writing of the reprimand."

He stopped. "I know your rights, detective." His exasperated tone revealed the interview's nature—a political joke.

Finally, she made the connection. "Henson."

He hobbled to her. "Henson. Saw you come in and called in all his favors to convene this interview. I don't know what he's up to, but if he weren't so good at ferreting out information, I'd have fired him the day after he started duty. He's a pain in the ass, but he's good."

"He's not internal affairs, he just wants my case. He wants to make a name for himself at my expense, and I'm not going to let him." Her anger manifested in a perfect cold, even burn, the kind that lasted and would feed the fight for hours.

She raised an eyebrow at the chief and motioned for him to lead the way. His eyes widened a moment then he led the way to the interview.

Like most conference rooms in offices, it held a long table surrounded by chairs in the middle of a rather nondescript room; the white walls interrupted only by a white dry erase board on the wall opposite the door. In front of the board, stationed at the head of the table, waited Henson. To his left sat a representative of internal affairs flipping through a packet of papers. To his right, folders were positioned like placemats in front of two chairs.

Refusing to play the game by his rules, she stalked to his chair. The chief said something as she moved, but she didn't hear. She focused only on Henson's smirk as she leaned close. "You want to make a name for yourself, you do it on your own." She didn't bother to whisper. "I've been told you're a good detective. Well, that's just fine. But you need to get something straight. If you want to work with me, you work *with* me. Intercepting my reports, spreading insidious rumors, and sabotaging my career to advance yours will not work in this precinct."

Henson's gaze darted to the man from internal affairs, who listened intently.

"My reputation is established here, as is my professionalism and integrity, so you can take your lies and walk if you have a problem with me." She stood slowly, eyes locked with Henson's.

When she faced the others, the chief rubbed his mustache vigorously, and though it obscured his mouth, it didn't hide the mirth in his eyes.

Finally, she faced the man from internal affairs, whom she didn't know. *He must be new. Oh, great. I'm sure that part about being established must have gone over well.* Making sure none of the doubt showed on her face, she waited for him to speak.

He took a moment, studying her. Then he extended a hand. "Detective, your reputation precedes you."

She nearly cringed as she shook his hand.

"I'm Edward Arrington, internal affairs." He reached into the breast pocket of his suit coat. "If you need my services . . . " He glanced at Henson with distaste. "Give me a call."

Henson sputtered. "She's sleeping with a suspect. She's let the Butcher get away three times." He came across as a child pleading with his parents for a later bedtime. "How can you let her keep a case she's mishandled so badly?"

Ignoring the tantrum, she turned to the chief. "Sir, I'd like to bring you up to speed with my findings so far."

And at his nod, she followed him out of the room, leaving Henson whining at the weary Arrington.

*

Ryan settled into a folding metal chair at a heavy wooden table set in the center of the archive room. Surrounding him stood rows of floor-to-ceiling file cabinets. In this room, the newspaper stored all excess pictures and notes for their stories from the past four decades.

For years, rumors abounded that the archives would be converted to digital data files, but until they completely filled the room, the powers that be would not foot the money needed for such a project.

Writers of most other papers kept their own notes, and the photographers their own pictures. However, at the *Daily Times*, the data came here, available to all writers and editors. He never knew when he would need new material to do a 'through the years' story.

It took Ryan a while to find the article archived in microfiche, and notes and unused photos for the accident that killed Robert Cooper. He'd worked with this system as long as he'd worked for the *Times*, and although others ranted about the inefficient storage, Ryan enjoyed digging through the files. He smiled, finding it almost as fun as digging for treasure.

He opened a folder on the table and read the reporter's notes. Not much on the slip of paper that didn't appear in the article, so he lifted a stack of pictures.

The original photo, run with the newspaper article, showed wreckage down a hillside through foliage. Even in black–and–white, it appeared impressive. Metal twisted at all angles, and the shattered windshield rolled over what was left of the roof.

The rest of the pictures showed specific close-ups of the car and surrounding bushes. Ryan set aside the ones he thought would interest Lydia.

In the first photo, the front bumper wrapped partway around the mangled trunk of the tree that halted its descent. Not particularly relevant. He set the photo in the folder.

In the next, blood glistened on leaves and roots of a nearby tree. *Most likely where Cooper fell when he was thrown from the car. This might be something.*

Snapped branches from the fall impaled the vinyl back of both front seats. Wicked. He took a long look before discarding it into the folder.

The last picture seemed taken to finish off the roll. From the haphazard angle and the awkward lighting, it appeared snapped while the photographer walked from the scene.

There in the dirt, on the edge of the road, appeared footprints. *Too large and too oddly shaped to be human.* Although the edges of the image suffered bad blurring, the center showing the print looked only remotely fogged. Lydia needed this one.

He worked at gathering everything together when his phone rang. Lydia. "Hello, gorgeous."

"Yeah, yeah" came the amused reply. "We'll be out front in a minute. Did you find anything?"

"Yup. Just putting the rest of the pictures back."

"Bring the whole thing."

"You want to look at all of it?"

"Absolutely. We might see something in them that you don't."

He enjoyed her confidence and suppressed his injured pride. "Whatever. Be down in a sec." He hung up, put everything in the folder and left. He stopped at a desk and signed out the folder.

As he walked out the front door, Lydia pulled to the curb. "Perfect timing," she said as he climbed into the back.

"Hey, babe." Ryan squeezed her shoulder, pretending to just notice Adams in the passenger seat. "Oh, you're still here." Then he leaned forward. "Where to now?"

"Let's go to your place and go over what you found."

*

Ryan spread the photographs on the coffee table. Lydia and Adams examined them with magnifying glasses while he read them the article and reporter's notes.

When he finished, she snorted. "About as much in the newspaper's account as there is in the police report. Seems everyone wanted to dismiss this as a normal car accident."

"People only see what they want."

She intently examined the picture in her hand.

"What do you see?" Ryan felt stirrings of desire. Even before she'd transformed, he knew this woman complemented him. Now they were beyond perfect for one another. *I want her to meet my family.* The stray idea startled him and drew him to the moment. He cleared his throat and sipped some of his coffee.

She glanced at him. "This may have been an accident at the start, but it wasn't normal." She pointed to one of the images she'd arranged on the table. "There are claw marks on the back of the front seats. And if you look closely at that one, the floor seems to shine."

"And being that the carpet is maroon, and the car was mangled—"

"It's possible that the investigating officer overlooked the amount of blood because injuries were expected." She tapped a fingernail on the table. "Here's what I think happened. I bet they picked up . . . " Her voice trailed off as she looked at Adams.

"Okay, here it comes," he said. "Tell me what's really happening here. What's with all the animal evidence?"

*

Almost from the time she found out what she'd become, Lydia wondered how she would tell Adams.

She glanced at Ryan to see if he had an opinion on how she should tell the man who now stood in the middle of the room with his arms crossed, glaring at both of them. Ryan responded with a shrug.

Okay, fine. This was her problem and he'd stay out of it for now. Great. *We're werewolves. No. Remember the dog DNA? No, shit.* Adams tilted his head. *Ah, crap.*

"Sit down, damn it. You're making me nervous," she snapped. When Adams didn't move, she stood her ground. "I said sit." She pointed to a chair.

Once he sat, she began to pace and decided to start at the beginning. "You remember the blood when you came to get me in the woods?" Only a nod in response. Okay. "The night before, I'd been attacked." She paused. "Attacked by a werewolf."

After a minute, he nodded. "Sure, makes sense. You know my father is a vampire and my mother is a banshee. You know, I think Fairweather is a leprechaun."

"Oh, shut the hell up," Ryan said as he picked up the magnifying glass and examined the pictures.

Lydia took advantage of the stunned silence. "It explains how Miller escaped when his house was in flames from the raid. The dog hairs we found at the scene. The canine DNA we found on Ms. Lenz. The attack patterns on all of his victims." She drew in a breath. "And what happened to Jacobs and me."

"What?" Adams squeaked and jumped from his chair as if

spikes started to protrude from the cushion.

"I handled the change better though. With Ryan's help." She laid a hand on Ryan's shoulder. "He's gone through it, too."

Horrified, Adams shifted his gaze between them while backing toward the window.

"Jesus, would you stop acting like we're going to rip your head off?" Lydia's voice cracked like a whip, stopping him in his tracks. "Okay, in a nutshell. A werewolf bites you then you turn into one. If you make it through your first full moon without killing a human, the urge to kill people goes away."

Ryan stood and wrapped an arm around her. "Lydia just graduated."

"Congratulations," Adams muttered and sat. He ran a hand through his hair and slouched in the recliner.

"I know it's hard to process, but you had to know the answer would have been difficult to take."

Adams slouched and closed his eyes. "So, both of you are *werewolves*. And the Butcher, Virgil Miller, he's one too." It wasn't a question and he didn't look at her nod. "So, okay." He took a deep breath, as if steeling himself to look at them then raised his head. "So, what do we do? Use a silver bullet?"

"Actually, we've been doing research, and silver anything is good." Lydia smiled and sat on the couch, pleased he made the attempt to understand. "A werewolf heals quickly from normal wounds. An injury inflicted by something silver causes a wound to heal in human time."

Ryan gave a curt nod. "So, stab with a steel knife, it heals right up. Stab with a silver knife, he bleeds like a human."

"Okay, I want some silver bullets." Adams smacked his hands together. "Damned if I'm getting close enough to use a knife."

Chapter 21

They planned strategy and discussed the reality of werewolves late into the night. When Lydia's eyelids started to close by themselves, she told Adams to meet them in the morning and they'd go weapon shopping.

Once Ryan closed the door, she lifted her hands to the only man she'd ever surrender to. "Let's go to bed."

As he scooped her into his arms, he whispered, "Are you really tired?" His gruff voice sent shivers through her body.

"Not anymore."

*

Once outside, Adams waved for a cab. As the vehicle pulled to the curb, he heard a growl. Spinning, he opened the door and fell into the seat, scanning for the noise. He pushed his emotions aside, every bit of police instinct coming to the fore. Bounding down the stairs of the next stoop came a flash of white. Cold as ice, he trained his weapon on the charging object.

Bellowing laughter of the cab driver filled the air as a toy poodle barked frantically at Adams, nipping and tearing at his pant leg. He kicked, and the little dog backed up enough for him to close the door. An elderly Asian woman scurried after and scooped the dog into her arms.

Adams leaned into the seat and struggled to catch his breath. For a second, he'd imagined the Butcher bounding toward him to rip out his throat. As the moment, and the cabby's laughter, faded, Adams realized what a fool he'd appeared.

He cleared his throat. "Whenever you catch your breath, West Sixteenth Street."

*

The shop Ryan suggested was located in a shack of a building on the highway just outside the city. It specialized in military weaponry, but they had a variety of novelty items as well.

"Bullets," Adams muttered hotly, glaring through the glass display case at the selection of knives.

Lydia exchanged a glance with Ryan, clapped the agitated sergeant on the back and smiled at the clerk. The lanky man would look more at home in a pair of overalls than the camouflage vest that seemed to be the store's uniform. Strawberry–blonde curls topped his head, with the same colored scruff lining his square jaw. His skin was reddened and flakey, as if he'd spent too much time in the sun recently. He only needed a straw hat and a sprig of hay in his teeth. To top it all off, the nametag on his vest read 'Billy Bob.'

"Hi. Uh . . . " She paused, simply unable to call him Billy Bob. "I would like some silver bullets for a display case. We're setting up a retirement gift for one of the officers down at the precinct."

"Got a silver–plated Glock twenty-two to go with them," Adams added, looking up from the case of knives.

"That's a new one," Billy Bob said. "Most of the time, folks ask for silver bullets to go werewolf huntin'."

"Werewolves?" Lydia forced an easy grin. "Can't get too many of them around here."

"No, can't say as we do." He stared at her for a bit. Then, as though satisfied by what he read in her eyes, he nodded once and went into the back.

"What?" Adams turned to Ryan. "He has them in stock?"

"I got a smelter back here," came a voice from the other room. "Just like doin' it. Got silver, gold, brass, aluminum—crap." They heard boxes fall.

Lydia called. "You okay?"

He came around the corner. "Yeah, got too much piled back there. Get an avalanche every now and then." He set a plastic tub filled with silver bullets on the counter in front of them. "There, how's that?"

They each chose a bullet and examined it. The craftsmanship was superb. "You put a lot of time into these," Lydia observed.

"It's a hobby." The clerk glowed at the compliment.

"How much to part with thirty?" Lydia asked.

The thin man scratched at his stubble. "Being as they are silver, and the work involved, how about two hundred?"

Before Lydia could accept, Ryan said, "One-twenty-five."

A light seemed to come on in the clerk's eyes. "Ah, but she already remarked on the quality. Smooth. They'll fire clean. One-seventy-five."

"But she won't be firing them. They'll sit in a display case." Ryan moved to the counter.

Lydia's breath came faster and her mouth went dry. She could see how much Ryan enjoyed himself. How crazy was it for her to get turned on by it?

No sooner had she finished the thought than he glanced over his shoulder and winked. She almost laughed as she fingered the pendant around her neck. *Got him riled too? Hmm . . . file that away for later.*

Billy Bob countered with, "One-fifty."

Ryan stretched out a hand. "Done."

Lydia bumped her hip against Ryan's as she scooted him aside to choose the bullets and hand the clerk her card. She glanced at Adams to tell him to get in there and pick some out too, but his expression stalled her.

He'd gone pale, his wide eyes staring at his cell phone. She took the phone from his hand and read the text message aloud. "Found him." Her pulse quickened, and she scrolled for the address. Signing the receipt, she pocketed the bag of bullets and led Adams out of the shop by the arm.

She spun him around and stared into his terrified features. "I won't blame you if you wanted to sit this one out. This is more than we signed on for when we joined the force." In a way, she hoped he would bow out. He didn't have the speed or agility to face this type of criminal.

He gulped, struggling with his fear. Suddenly, Ryan stood beside her and grabbed Adams by his shirtfront, growling inches from his face.

"Shit!" Adams punched Ryan in the face and scrambled over the car hood, drawing his weapon.

Ryan turned and kissed her cheek. "Okay, your friend can come."

Unable to stop a grin, she climbed into the car. Ryan took his place in the back and they both waited until Adams straightened, brushed himself off and got in.

"So," Lydia said once they were on the road. "Ready to go or do we need to stop off for a change of clothes?"

"Yeah, yeah. You immortals are real funny," Adams said and reached into his pocket and withdrew a small medallion and fastened the chain around his neck. "Can't hurt," he said when she gave him a look. Then he released the clip from his weapon, emptying the bullets into his lap. He held out a hand and she passed him the bag and her weapon.

She drove in silence, the only noise inside the car the ticks as Adams filled their magazines. Excitement bubbled in her chest.

She'd watched for months as this murderer killed without discrimination. Getting close only to have him escape. Even if he hadn't changed her, it would have become personal. The hunt had gone on too long, the deaths too numerous and mutilations too complete for any detective to stay detached.

Her first impulse was to reach for the radio and call it in. Get backup out to the building, just in case. But she dismissed the thought before her hand left the steering wheel. Extra forces would have regular bullets not able to kill him, resulting in more police deaths and Miller escaping again.

He couldn't get past her this time. The three of them were the only ones who knew Miller's true nature. They would not bother trying to bring him in. Nobody would try to capture a rabid animal. They'd kill it.

Adams handed over her gun, and she holstered it. They turned into the commerce park, an area of town filled with warehouses. Aside from signage, buildings were almost indistinguishable from one another.

Tan brick raised two stories, topped with flat roofs. Loading docks opened like gaping mouths out of the sides of the buildings. She could see workers inside some of the buildings moving cargo.

They sought a warehouse abandoned by the newspaper. It didn't take long. The windows of the office sported boards, and the doors to the docks stood closed.

Lydia drove past and pulled into the lot of a beer distributor next door. They exited and gathered by the trunk.

She turned to Adams. "I'll be honest, I don't want you here." When he started to say something, she raised a hand. "But if you stay hidden, Ryan and I can distract him until you can get off a shot."

Ryan nodded in agreement. "We'll go first and you follow after five minutes."

"But you don't have a weapon," Adams observed.

Without a word, and seemingly from nowhere, two sliver knives appeared in Ryan's grip. Then with a flick, they disappeared just as quickly.

"Cool." The sergeant nodded approval and clapped them both on the back before turning to sit in the car to wait.

Ryan took her hand as they started toward bushes that separated the lots. Amazed by Ryan's show of knives, she struggled not to gasp like a schoolgirl.

He aroused desire in her with the minutest actions. At the moment, she wanted to take him into the bushes and make wild passionate love. *Later.*

"I'll hold you to that." Ryan didn't look in her direction, but the feeling that radiated from him was almost too much to bear. She stopped and gripped his face in both hands, kissing him hard.

When she broke the kiss, she clamped down on emotions

skipping around in her heart and said, "We have a job to do."

All the passion emanating from him ceased. Even so, the sense of completion still comforted her as they crossed through a gap in the bushes. With her own thoughts and emotions under control, she could sense something else. A primal hunger. Unsatisfied desire. Ryan's nod in her peripheral vision let her know he sensed it too.

Together they walked to a concrete staircase at the rear of the building. The doorway gaped at the top; a chunk of door ripped from the hinges and lay in splinters to the side of the stairs.

Lydia drew her weapon. She climbed first, sliding in sideways. She dropped into the dark then leaped to the side in one fluid motion. Ryan joined her. They stood still, breathing only slightly and allowing their eyes to adjust to the dark.

Before her stood a large pallet of newspapers. Not neatly folded, they seemed gathered for recycling. She figured they'd sat there since the company abandoned the warehouse.

She and Ryan moved slowly across the concrete floor, stepping with care to make only the faintest noise. Around the first pallet, more lined the space. It seemed the warehouse overflowed with them. When she finished here, she'd have to find whom to cite with the fire hazard.

A scream pierced the silence. A wave of joy followed. From the depths of darkness, whimpering echoed. Lydia increased the pace. The Butcher didn't torture his victims. The fact that he did it now made stealth irrelevant.

She smelled the sweet metallic scent of fresh blood as they drew closer to the noises.

"God!" a man's voice cried out in agony.

A deep chuckle filled with menace rumbled toward them.

When they rounded another pallet, they moved into a pool of light made by one of the few skylights in the aluminum roof.

On his back in the center of the light lay Adams, a gash across his chest, his limbs broken and splayed at odd angles. His gun remained holstered at his side.

Over him crouched Virgil Miller, his ragged clothes coated with dirt and sprayed with blood. Without hesitation, she fired a shot. Though the first bullet hit him in the shoulder, the grotesque man barely moved from the impact. He dashed behind a pallet on the other side of the clearing. Two bullets lodged in the papers before she stopped firing.

She ran to Adams, gun still in hand. He struggled to speak, spitting blood and gasping for air. "Cornered me. Bushes." He coughed then grinned, his teeth colored with blood. "Get him. I'll hold here."

"Shit." She stood to tell Ryan to take Adams to the car and found him gone. She stepped around her old friend and started down the passage where Miller disappeared.

As she neared the edge of the second pallet, a roar split the quiet in front of her. A body flew past. Ryan landed, tossed like a rag doll, knives clattering from his hands.

She rounded the corner and got off another two shots. She could only make out shadow, but a whine told her she hit her mark before he ducked around another corner.

She ran to Ryan. He stood, albeit wobbly, knives once again in his hands. "I got him in the arm and chest," he panted. "But not deep enough."

Another cry from Adams had them racing his way. This time, his face was slashed and an eye hung from its socket. Mercifully, he'd fallen into unconsciousness.

"Why?" Lydia roared to the rafters.

The reply came from a gruff voice directly in front of her. "You know the terror is almost as satisfying as the flesh." He stepped into the light. His large nose barely shadowed the white teeth grinning at her.

"I wanted you, you know." As he paced to the right, she matched his movement with her weapon. "That's why I made you."

She suppressed a shudder of disgust and fired again, just as

Ryan leapt onto Miller from above. She screamed in horror as the bullet entered her love, and he crumpled in a heap. Miller stood and brushed himself off. "Thank you."

"No!" she screamed and closed the distance. The world shattered. Like breaking through thin ice of a pond, her flesh burned, submerged in freezing fear.

Ignoring the vile killer, she cradled Ryan's face in her hands. It couldn't be. She bowed her head and rocked over him. The silver pendant swung between them as she swayed, seeming to glow.

"That's enough of that." A clawed hand gripping her shoulder, he wrenched her from Ryan's body.

She grasped the silver leaf in her fist. He spun her to face him and pressed his revolting body against hers. One of his hands clenched her throat while the other ripped at her jeans.

"You're mine now." He leaned in, his dripping tongue reached for her face.

"I want you," she said hotly, running her left hand up his arm to grip his shoulder. "To die." She dug her nails into the back of his neck and pierced his juggler with her pendant.

He staggered, clutching his gurgling throat. Her blood ran cold. No malice, no rage, just the detachment of justice well done. She wouldn't have to worry about this monster infecting anyone else.

Although her infection became a blessing, she would never wish it on anyone. Too much could have gone wrong. How many others did he infect before her, hopeless souls with no one to help them through their first full moon? She could tell by the gurgle coming from the beast, she didn't want to know.

She stalked to Adams and took his gun. Miller tried to escape between the stacks, and she merely followed less than three steps behind.

Tiring of the slow chase, she kicked him in the back and sprawled the weakening werewolf on the ground.

"Please," he implored with a whimper, reaching for her.

She snorted. "Give me a break." She unloaded the clip into Virgil

Miller at point blank range. Drained and detached, she stared at the remnants of the Bestial Butcher's head. "Well, at least I destroyed his brain," she said to the empty warehouse.

When she returned to the clearing, she found Ryan struggling to sit. Her heart swelled and she gasped. Tears fell unbidden down her cheeks. From this angle, she could see where the bullet had exited his shoulder, a through–and–through just below his collarbone.

She ripped off her sleeve and pressed hard to quench the bleeding. Flipping open her cell phone, she called for an ambulance.

Adams moaned, his limbs twitching uselessly. Ryan placed his hand on hers and kept pressure on his shoulder while she went to kneel beside Adams.

"Just a moment, they'll be here soon," she said gently, stroking his hair, reassuring him until the paramedics could be heard at the entrance. She ran to the doors and kicked through the lock to give them entrance.

Once they loaded Adams onto a stretcher, she crossed to where Ryan sat bare-chested while another paramedic placed a bandage on his shoulder.

"You may still need stitches," said the technician. He slipped the arm in a sling. "Don't move it." The paramedic turned as Lydia approached. "You're with him?" At her nod, he said, "Make sure he sees a doctor tomorrow."

"I will," she managed past a throat gone tight with emotion. The paramedic helped Ryan to his feet then went to assist with Adams' gurney.

Her lip quivered as she stared into the eyes of the only man she'd ever loved. "I thought I'd lost you," she whispered.

"Never," he said. "We're immortal, darling, and wolves mate for life."

About the Author

Born in Tennessee, Kristine Overbrook is a daughter of New England. She spent the first part of her life traveling the east coast as a navy brat. When her father left the navy, her family stayed in the Virginia Beach area. That's where she grew up, met her husband and started her family.

Kristine dabbled in writing for years until she began working with a woman who insisted she develop her inner writer. After much pestering, Kristine surrendered and enjoyed it so much she has indulged the writer within her ever since.

She currently lives in Pennsylvania with her family and two dogs.

In the mood for more Crimson Romance? Check out *Children of the Wolves* by Jessica Starre at CrimsonRomance.com.